SCREWED

POWERTOOLS: THE ORIGINAL CREW
RETURNS, BOOK 1

JAYNE RYLON

HAPPY ENDINGS PUBLISHING

V4

eBook ISBN: 978-1-947093-11-9

Print ISBN: 978-1-947093-12-6

Cover Design by Jayne Rylon

Editing by Mackenzie Walton

Proofreading by Fedora Chen

Formatting by Jayne Rylon

ABOUT THE BOOK

The original Powertools crew is back in a brand new series!

Joe has it all--a gorgeous wife, two amazing children, four best friends who are also sometimes lovers, and a booming construction business. He never expected to face some sort of midlife crisis. But somehow, he finds himself longing for even more.

How can he tell his family and the rest of the crew that he wishes they could be closer to his Uncle Tom and the rest of the Hot Rods and Hot Rides gangs?

An emergency crew meeting turns into a steamy attempt to show Joe exactly what he'd be missing out on if he left the crew and their polyamourous lifestyle behind. Will it work? Will he listen to his heart or parts of him below the belt? Either way, he's screwed.

This is a standalone book set in the Powertools universe. All your favorite Hot Rods and Hot Rides characters will be making appearances as well. So come make new book boyfriends or hang out with old ones.

ADDITIONAL INFORMATION

Sign up for the Naughty News for contests, release updates, news, appearance information, sneak peek excerpts, reading-themed apparel deals, and more. www.jaynerylon.com/newsletter

Shop for autographed books, reading-themed apparel, goodies, and more www.jaynerylon.com/shop

A complete list of Jayne's books can be found at www.jaynerylon.com/books

1

J oe tapped his fingers on the steering wheel of his truck. He stared at the last red light on the road separating himself from his bed, which hopefully contained his naked wife. He must be getting old —hell, he'd passed forty a couple years back—because the thought of falling asleep with Morgan snuggled in his arms was even more appealing than the thought of keeping her awake half the night.

He'd originally planned to get home before dinner, but drummed up every excuse he could think of to keep from leaving his uncle Tom and his cousin, Eli, and the place they'd built for themselves at Hot Rides in Middletown, a couple states over. Guilt ate at Joe. It wasn't like he didn't want to see his immediate family either. Morgan, their kids, and the rest of the crew. He'd missed each and every one of them.

Torn, he felt like no matter what he did lately, he was screwed.

Blinking hard at reality until his negative thoughts dissipated, Joe peered ahead to the apartment he'd shared with Morgan for the past thirteen years. It was perched above her bakery, Sweet Treats, which she'd made from scratch. Annoyed with himself for not arriving before his kids' bedtime, he studied the window of the room Nathan and Klea shared. Dark. Actually, there weren't any lights on. Not even the flickering glow of someone watching TV in his own bedroom.

It wasn't *that* late yet.

What the hell?

Joe's stomach cramped. What if something had happened to his family while he'd been away, acting like some confused teenager instead of doing his duty to protect them and provide for them like he should? He snatched his phone from the holder on the dash, where he'd been using it as a GPS, and speed-dialed Morgan.

Thankfully it wasn't more than a moment before she answered.

"Hey, cupcake. Is everything okay?"

"Yep." She sighed. "And it'll be even better when you get back."

"Thing about that, I'm pretty much here. Looking at the house now, but it doesn't seem like anyone's home. Where are you?"

"I'm up at Kayla and Dave's place. I thought you were heading up to the lake to talk to Mike and the rest of the crew about something?" Morgan asked, the background din of his friends talking and laughing growing fainter, as if she'd stepped onto the porch for some privacy.

"Decided not to tonight. I left later than I planned and I'm beat." He pinched the bridge of his nose, because it was so much more than the long drive or the manual labor he'd been putting in at his cousin's place that was causing his bones to feel like they were going to sink through his skin.

"Oh." Morgan didn't say so, but he could hear the disappointment in her voice. "Kate and I sort of got an overnight sitter for the kids. We've been holding off on eating until you arrived. Well, most of us. You know Dave can't resist a potluck for very long."

"Ah, shit. I didn't realize you had something planned." Joe kept fucking up. Springing for a babysitter for Nathan, Klea, Abby, and Landry meant the crew had been hoping for more than a simple meal together.

Alone time. Adult time. Sexy time.

They intended to welcome him home properly.

The construction crew made up of him and his five best friends did more than work together. They played together, too. Had for more than twenty years now. What kind of bastard was he that he was thinking about betraying them?

"I know how much you love surprises. So...*surprise*." No matter how off Joe was, or how weary, that coy flavor to Morgan's sugary voice had him perking up.

Fuck it. There was only so much temptation a man could resist. Even if he knew it wasn't the right thing to indulge in.

Joe checked his side and rearview mirrors to verify there was no one about but him before swinging his truck around in a U-turn. He accelerated toward the mountains and the place he belonged. He should have known better than to doubt it even for a moment. This was who he was and he couldn't change it. Not even if he wanted to. "Okay. I'm on my way."

"If you're not up for it—"

"I am. I always am." Whether Joe was trying to convince her or himself was debatable.

"There's my guy." Morgan laughed. He could picture her bright eyes as she did. "Hurry home, okay?"

Home. It wasn't their house she was waiting at. It was one of their best friends' places. But that didn't mean shit, because when you were part of the crew, home was where they were. And they all knew it.

Which meant the possibilities Joe had been mulling over the entire trip back from Middletown were even more preposterous than he'd already considered them. Thank God he hadn't rushed home and blurted them out without thinking about it some more.

No, tonight he was going to eat, laugh, fuck, and forget about dumb ideas that could only ruin the best things in his life.

2

Joe crept up the long, windy gravel road that snaked through the forest to the lodge at Bare Natural. The fact that his friends owned a booming naturist resort where guests could roam around the serene landscape in their birthday suits no longer even fazed him. A lot of things that might have once seemed impossible or outlandish to him now felt normal, because it was for them. It had been so long since he'd felt awkward about his sexuality or worried about censure that he'd grown comfortable.

If he left this bubble they'd created where they were safe and happy and prospering, he'd have to deal with shit he hadn't struggled with in years. And so would his wife and kids. He really must have temporarily lost his mind to even consider it. But when he'd sat at Hot Rides, talking to his uncle Tom, Eli, and their friends, none of these roadblocks had seemed insurmountable.

Joe blinked, trying to navigate his way along the path in the dark. The beam of his headlights glinted off animal eyes in the underbrush, which blanketed the ground between soaring pine trees. Though he knew every acre of this lakeside refuge, he still felt like he was trespassing on sacred ground.

But maybe that was because he knew how close he'd come to deserting his crew. The same people who were about to welcome him back with very warm, very open arms...among other things.

He clenched his jaw as the truck rolled over a few potholes left from the harsh winter, making a mental note to offer to help Dave fill them sometime soon. With his bum leg, jobs like that weren't always easy for him, but asking for help seemed even tougher.

That was how the crew worked, though. Each of them had their own strengths and weaknesses. Together they were unbreakable. United they could survive anything. On their own...not so much.

Joe would do well to remember that. Hell, without his partners he wouldn't even have the family he adored so much. They'd been there to make his first date with Morgan so special that she'd seen he was serious about building a life with her. And when they'd struggled to conceive, the guys had lent...well...something other than their *hands*.

He owed them everything. And he planned to let them fuck this midlife crisis right out of him.

Joe rolled into the clearing around Kayla and Dave's personal cabin, not far from the resort's lodge. He shut off the truck and sat there for a few moments. The familiar golden glow streaming through the floor-to-ceiling windows brightened the gloomy thoughts he'd mulled over for too many miles. Gray tendrils of smoke snaking into the air above the chimney made him sure the crew was safe and toasty warm inside, despite whatever they may or may not be wearing.

His knee cracked when he hopped down. His back ached, forcing him to stretch it out before he headed for the house, but those minor symptoms of his maturity weren't going to stop him from playing his part when he rejoined his friends. The more years they spent together, the better they got at taking care of each other, whatever that required.

It might have been selfish, but Joe was looking forward to letting go of responsibility and allowing them to settle him. He took the stairs to the porch two at a time, then entered without knocking, shutting the door quickly behind him to avoid letting in a brisk early spring breeze.

As eight faces turned in his direction, all with wide, glad smiles, he felt his muscles begin to relax. Especially when he caught sight of Morgan, who was lounging on the deep, shaggy rug in front of the fire with a glass of wine in her hand while wearing a silk robe. He licked his lips as he took in her shapely legs and the cleavage on display between her lapels.

"Damn, that looks good." Joe briefly eyed the buffet piled with food and then the group of naked people beyond it for far longer. "Is it all for me?"

"Guess we missed you. Lucky bastard." Mike's mouth tipped up on one side in his characteristic wry grin as he spread his arms. "What are you hungry for first?"

"No offense, Kate, but it isn't your world-famous mac and cheese." Joe could ignore the rumbling of his stomach, but all of a sudden he couldn't dismiss his need to be part of this group. To ground himself and remind himself where he truly belonged and to whom.

"Damn it. I told you guys he wouldn't care if I ate

without him." Dave pouted. "Those buffalo wings were calling my name."

"Just think, now you can work up an appetite and have room for more of them after you're done." Kayla distracted him with a brush of her hand across his mammoth pecs. His nipples were tight around the studs through them. After so many years together, Kayla's penchant for piercings and tattoos—not to mention strolling around in the nude—had rubbed off on her husband.

"Yeah, we were saving you from yourself," Neil teased, making Joe wince, since he needed them to do the same for him. "You wouldn't want to be full of greasy chicken or in a food coma when it came to the good stuff. Isn't there some kind of saying like that? No eating thirty minutes before an orgy?"

"I think they were talking about swimming." Mike laughed, his stare growing a lot more serious and steamier as he looked at his wife, Kate. Even all these years later, any time they talked about a pool party, every one of the crew flashed back to the fateful summer day they'd first bonded with Kate and made her one of their own. That moment had changed the course of their lives, steering them in the direction that had made each of them unbelievably happy. Joe should be ashamed of his greed. "But I'm sure someone would be willing to take care of Kayla for you if you'd rather pig out."

Dave practically purred as he stroked her hair. "You know, it might be worth it to watch her getting off on that. But I'm selfish. And starving. It's been too long."

He stared pointedly at Joe.

"Sorry," he muttered, and they knew it wasn't because he'd stayed longer than he'd intended in Middletown that day. It was more than that. Lately his head hadn't been in the game and he'd passed up a few other opportunities for a good time that he otherwise would have jumped on.

He was hurting his friends, his lovers, and he didn't intend to do that again that night. He planned to give them all of himself. As much as they would take.

"It's fine." Morgan was quick to shoot Dave a warning glare as she rose and passed him in order to cross to Joe. Her hair bounced, curling over her shoulders when she swiveled her head toward him again. The last thing Joe wanted was to come between the people he loved most. So he distracted her by opening his arms and wrapping her up in them.

"I missed you," he whispered, drawing a deep breath and letting the scent of her shampoo and light perfume fill his lungs. She was right there with him, her arms going around him equally as tight until they made one complete unit standing there together.

Though the night would certainly become more involved, a simple hug was exactly what he craved from her then.

What he had, what he'd found, was so damn special that the fact that he couldn't seem to appreciate it lately was making him feel like the shittiest partner in the world. He'd heard once that guilt was a useless emotion. Ironically, it didn't seem benign. It felt paralyzing.

As if she could hear the struggle in his heart—with her cheek mashed to his chest—Morgan grabbed his wrist, guiding his hand into the V of her robe. He felt her breath hitch, and looked down in time to spot her lick her lower lip. Desire, simple and familiar, swelled inside him, pushing aside everything else.

Joe cupped Morgan's face in his hands, hoping she

didn't notice his fingers trembling as he tipped it up. He lowered his head and sealed their mouths, drawing strength from her even as he fed her his own pent-up frustration, released by their mutual desire.

It was always like this. She had the power to transform even the most ragged of his emotions into something beautiful and sweet for them both to gorge on. Joe nudged her robe aside until her chest was fully bared to him, then froze. The delicate gold chain draped around her neck and between her breasts made her skin look even more flawless than it was. He traced the fine metal down to the setting that dangled from it, swirling around a rock. Not a diamond, but a simple pebble.

From the date that had started it all for them.

The one he'd taken from the pumpkin patch the night he'd known without a doubt that they were made for each other. Had he gotten so used to being incredibly fortunate —with a successful business, a loving family, a spicy sex life, and the best friends a guy could hope for, that he was willing to sacrifice it all for one tiny thing he couldn't have otherwise?

What the hell was wrong with him? *Welcome to your midlife crisis, dumbass.*

"You okay?" Morgan murmured against his cheek when he paused. "We can go home if you'd rather."

"You were right. This *is* home." He rested his forehead on hers for a moment before lifting his head and staring at their friends, gathered around them, their expressions ranging from curious to downright concerned.

"Sorry, guys. Sorry." He scrunched his eyes closed, then stared at Mike, hoping the other man would understand what he craved when he said, "Be my foreman tonight."

"You sure?" Mike arched one brow. He crossed his arms and spread his feet. There was a reason the man had been the unofficial leader of their crew for decades. This was who he was and what he did best. Tonight, Joe wasn't ashamed to admit he needed that.

Joe nodded.

Morgan smiled softly, then kissed him. As she preoccupied him, Mike stepped up behind them. He put his hands on Joe's shoulders. Compared to his wife's, Mike's fingers felt huge and solid. As strong but without the finesse and grace of Morgan's touch.

It was raw and perfect.

Mike held him, steadied him, as Joe poured his feelings into the kiss he shared with Morgan. Heat enveloped Joe from behind and in front. His hands began to wander, filling with the supple flesh he knew as well as his own. Morgan sighed. Was she relieved? Had she assumed he would back out or fail her?

Not tonight. Hopefully, not ever.

"Kate, come here," Mike called to his wife.

When she approached, shucking her robe—which matched Morgan's—she put her hands on Mike's abs—in the gap between them and Joe's lower back—surrounding him in her embrace from behind. As the sound of her kissing some part of Mike, probably his shoulder, reached into Joe's mind, he felt her knuckles grazing the spot just above his ass. "What do you need, Mike?"

"Get rid of my shorts and find me some lube, please."

As Joe shuddered, Kate purred her appreciation for what she was about to watch. She got off on seeing her husband go all dominant on them. Mike gripped Joe tighter and Morgan slipped her tongue between his lips when he moaned in response.

"Okay, damn it. You guys were right. This was worth waiting for," Dave grumbled from the couch in front of the fire where his wife, Kayla, was curled up beside him. He took his impressive cock in hand and gave it a few idle strokes. On his other side was Neil with Devon already in his lap. The man they shared, James, was seated on the floor between their knees. His head tipped back so that he could look up adoringly at his husband and wife.

"I told you, Dave. Everyone's going to be satisfied before the night is over. Be patient." James reached out to the side and patted Dave's shin. It said something that he wasn't wearing anything—not even a blanket covered up the scars on his legs, which snaked even that low on his limb. He didn't flinch when James touched it either. Not anymore.

The gruesome accident he'd survived had left its mark, one that hadn't entirely faded, even after all this time.

Another knot in Joe's gut loosened as he realized that this wasn't only for him. It was for each of them. When one of them was stressed or sick or struggling with something, every one of them felt it. Relief coursed through the entire room, reflecting back as heat and longing.

While they talked, Kate worked. Joe knew she'd done as Mike asked when the other man's cock sprang free and prodded his ass where it met his thigh. "Fuck, are you sure you haven't grown since the last time we did this?"

Morgan chuckled and patted Joe's chest, as if telling him he could take it. And he would. He'd love every second of it when Mike fit himself inside of Joe's ass and reminded him of his place on the crew and in life.

"It's probably just that it's been a while." Mike raked

his teeth over Joe's neck, making his own cock stiffen.

There was a hint of desperation to their interactions that gave what they were doing an edge. One he hadn't felt in a while. It was scary, yeah. But it was also exciting.

Morgan sank to her knees and did for him what Kate had done for Mike. She unbuttoned his jeans, then stripped them off along with his boots, underwear, and socks. While she was there, she paused, set one hand on his bunched quadriceps and took him into her mouth, making white heat flash across his mind.

She knew exactly how to please him, and—even better—how to tease. She didn't suck, but ran her tongue along the underside of his shaft, getting him steely hard before pulling off and placing a kiss on the tip. As she did, Mike grabbed the bottom of his long-sleeved shirt and tugged it over his head. "You won't be needing this."

Nope. He definitely would not. Joe couldn't wait for every inch of his skin to be pressed to someone he loved, who would keep him safe, even from himself.

Morgan got to her feet and wrapped her hand around his cock, encouraging him to thrust into her loose fist before she used her grip to lead him deeper into the cabin Kayla and Dave had made their home. When the rug smooshed soft between his toes, Morgan stopped and sat at his feet.

Her hand wasn't the only thing urging him to follow. Along with Joe's own desire, Mike pushed on his shoulders, making it clear that he wanted Joe to join his wife.

"Lie down, Morgan," Mike commanded. "I need you to keep his mind off what I'm doing for a few minutes."

"That's not going to be a problem." She stretched out, cupping her breasts as she held his rapt attention. Joe blanketed her as they became the main attraction for the couple and throuple cheering them on from the sidelines.

"Mike's going to fuck him so good." James sighed. "I wish it was me acting weird lately so someone would have to set me straight."

"We can pretend later," Neil teased. Of all of them, James was the most submissive and the most attracted to other men.

"I like that plan. If you're still up for it..." James laughed as Devon ruffled his hair and leaned down for a kiss of her own. She loved watching Neil and James together nearly as much as she loved being sandwiched between them.

Their familiar banter set Joe at ease as he settled himself between his wife's thighs. The fit of her against him, the ultimate security the crew instilled him, all of it was so familiar and so right, he couldn't think about anything else. Especially not about making changes that would put moments like this in jeopardy.

Joe got lost in kissing Morgan. Tenderly at first, then more urgently as they began to grind on each other. And when she shifted so that her pussy straddled his thigh, he realized how ready she was for him. For all of them.

"I'm sorry I kept you waiting," he panted between brushes of their lips against each other.

"I wasn't upset. I knew you would make it up to me." She moaned softly as he rocked against her. It meant something that she had that much confidence in him. More than he had in himself sometimes. Okay, most of the time. Morgan always believed in him the way he believed in her, without reservation, and that's why they'd lasted as long as they had. Why they'd make it through anything, he hoped.

He brushed her hair aside to kiss her neck, then her collarbones and back up to her mouth. When he shifted, so did his cock. It nudged Morgan's core. She gasped. Slick heat enveloped his dick.

"Welp, that's that. No way can he resist now." Dave laughed as Joe nearly blacked out from anticipation. They knew him well.

At the same time, he understood them. Though he didn't have the excess brain cells to fire back some smartass reply, Devon did it for him. "Like you could either? Come on, we know the instant Kayla stops teasing you both by rubbing your back and decides she wants some D, you won't be able to hold out either."

Joe glanced to the side, nodding at Dave.

As if to prove her best friend right, Kayla refocused her attention from the lazy massage she'd been giving Dave as she observed Joe and Morgan—as well as Kate and Mike—getting warmed up to baiting Dave with some enticement of his own.

She leaned in and licked his nipple, biting lightly on it before flicking the piercing there with the tip of her tongue.

"Shit. Fine," he growled. "But we all know I'm the weak link. Joe's usually not."

Was that what he'd become? A liability to them? Maybe.

Joe's cock lost a bit of its stiffness.

"He's still not. None of you are." Mike slapped Joe's flank, making his dick drive a bit deeper into the opening of Morgan's pussy. Her heat and slickness lured him in. Fuck yes. Whether he deserved it or not—her or them or their respect—he was going to take what they were offering and love every moment of it.

3

Joe groaned, then sank the rest of the way into his wife.

Morgan cried out his name and clutched his shoulders, not so differently from how Mike had. Except somehow it seemed like she was using the grip to ground herself when Mike had clearly been doing that for Joe. She relied on him to give her strength and he wanted to be the man she expected him to be.

For one brief moment, he felt the old trauma rise up inside him from the days when he'd been unable to get her pregnant. All the feelings about not being enough for her tried to riot inside him.

"Um, Mike," Kayla warned. Figured, she had the best view of his expression from her position at Dave's side and she was also one of the most intuitive of their group. "Don't give Joe too much time to think. Hurry up and get your cock in him. He needs you."

Morgan dragged her nails down Joe's back, forcing him to focus on her even as Mike kneed Joe's legs wider apart to make room for himself between them. That's when Joe heard the familiar glide of slippery gel on flesh. Mike was getting himself lubed up and ready to do exactly as Joe had asked.

The thought of being joined with the other man, even as they both rode Morgan, made Joe jerk. He burrowed deeper into his wife, a little harder with that thrust. She didn't seem to mind, instead arching to meet him and raising her legs to wrap them around his hips. Her heels rested on the top swell of his ass before she peeked up for guidance from Mike.

"You're fine. I can get to everything I need from here." Mike proved his point by spreading Joe's ass apart, making his hole clench at the wash of cooler air over the sensitive skin. He knelt there, upright and began to tap his dick against Joe's flesh even as Joe worked himself balls-deep in Morgan.

Fuck. How could it get better than this?

He wasn't sure, but it did when Mike barked at him to relax an instant before he pressed his thumb to Joe's hole and began to rub in circles timed to the short strokes Joe made into Morgan.

"Damn, that's hot. Isn't it?" Neil asked someone.

Joe figured it was Devon when she answered, "Mmm, yep."

"James, why don't you tell me how much our wife likes watching two men fuck?" Neil suggested.

"Put your dick in my ass and I'll let you know," the other man retorted.

"Maybe later. If you're good." Neil knew as well as the rest of them that James liked to be teased first. It made him come ten times as hard to be denied for a while. How he had the self-restraint, Joe had no idea. Because if he hadn't already been smothered in Morgan's pussy, he'd have died. He was pretty sure.

Morgan smiled up at him, then bit his lip, as if telling him she felt the same way.

So James did the next best thing. He turned around, his foot touching Joe's calf as he buried his face in his wife's pussy where she sat on their husband's lap.

The sexy noises Devon made as James pleased her were only more fuel added to the fire burning hotter in Joe than the real one blazing nearby. And when he was so damn turned on he was afraid he might ruin everything by coming too soon, he felt the pressure at his ass increase.

Mike's dick fit against him, then began to work him open.

Joe groaned. The foreman's hand came around his throat and held him steady as he invaded Joe's ass.

"Yeah." Mike grunted as he wedged himself deeper. "Take it, Joe. Take me. Remember whose crew you're on."

Oh, he fucking knew it. Mike's cock was making it obvious as it advanced, piercing Joe's resistance and driving him forward so that he fit even tighter inside his own wife. Morgan moaned, hugging him with her arms, legs, and pussy as Mike began to screw him.

Joe relished the weight of Mike pinning him down, making sure he stayed put and couldn't run. That he didn't ruin the best things he had in life by wanting to bolt. It was like the world's most muscular security blanket, keeping him there, fused tight to his wife, surrounded by the people he loved most in the world.

Morgan seemed to get off on the extra pressure even more than Joe did. She called his name, then Mike's, and squirmed beneath them, rocking her hips upward to match Joe stroke for stroke. She fucked him in time to the foreman, both of them working together to blow Joe's mind. And it was working.

He trembled between them.

"That's so sexy, Mike." Kate hummed, spreading her legs as she began to touch herself. If Joe could have reached, he'd have done it for her, slipping his fingers into her tightness. But he couldn't, and right then, the only thing he could think of was holding on as long as possible.

Mike didn't even have to ask for assistance. He shot a glance at Neil without ever breaking his rhythm, pumping into Joe's ass hard and deep. The other man obeyed the silent command, leaving his wife and husband with a lingering kiss for each in order to take care of one of their own.

That's how they operated.

No one was left behind. No one was forgotten.

Neil sank to the floor and rested his back on the couch beside James and Devon, then lifted Kate into his lap so they were seated with her back pressed to his chest. He lowered her gently so that her legs slipped over his and his cock aligned with her core.

"You want him inside you?" Mike asked his wife. "Fucking you like I'm fucking Joe?"

Joe groaned, his balls drawing up tighter to his body as Mike's urgent thrusts pressed Joe deeper within Morgan than he could have managed to get on his own.

Together they were better than apart.

He couldn't forget that. Wouldn't.

Thinking of his foolishness, Joe retreated from the edge of release. He took in what everyone else was doing, watching Kate kiss Neil. It wasn't often that she played with someone other than Mike, so it was a special treat to watch them make out even as she reached between Neil's legs and aimed his cock at her opening.

"Go ahead," she told him.

Neil grabbed her hips and guided her onto his length, sheathing his cock in her body with one long stroke that made Kate's head fall back onto his shoulders. He cupped her breasts and put her on display for Mike. The man must have liked what he saw because his dick got even fatter and harder in Joe's ass.

"Fuck yes!" Mike roared. "I can't wait to see her come all over you and drag you with her."

Kate whimpered, "Not yet. Feels too good. We're just getting started."

Mike grinned at her. "I love it when you're greedy. Ride him, baby."

So she did. Meanwhile, Devon teased James. "You should see him, fucking her. You know how much he gets off on being buried in a nice, tight pussy. Almost as much as he's going to love being in your ass later. You know that, right?"

James reached down and stroked his own cock without pausing whatever magic he was working with his mouth long enough to respond. Devon leaned forward and brushed his hand aside to stroke him herself. He didn't always get off on fucking as much as he did being fucked. Fortunately that worked for her too. She loved taking control of her husband and using him exactly as they both liked. She might have been the smallest of them all, but there was no doubt she was the most fierce.

Devon had been a member of the crew for more than a decade. She worked as hard as any of the guys on their job sites—hell, even more, to prove that she deserved her spot in their company. It wasn't necessary, but even now it seemed to matter to her that she never took the easy road.

She stood up abruptly, stealing James's treat.

"Please, Devon. Let me eat you." He strained his neck for another taste, but she dodged him.

"Dave, Kayla, can we have the couch?" She looked at her friends, who'd advanced to stroking each other as they made out. They grinned as they moved to the floor, both kneeling as they never stopped kissing and ended up near Joe and Morgan's heads.

With plenty of room, Devon shoved James onto his back, then straddled his head, facing his feet. She petted his chest and abs as she settled onto his mouth, smothering him with her sweet pussy and watching his cock jump as she did it.

Neil groaned and thrust up into Kate twice as hard as he saw his lovers teasing each other. Despite how well he was filling Kate, they all knew he'd be good for another round or two. Whatever it took to wear out his playful mates after they'd gotten each other warmed up.

Devon leaned forward and took James' cock into her mouth. She slid down it until her lips rested at the base of his shaft before reaching out to play with his balls while she sucked.

He jerked beneath her and must have redoubled his efforts, because she moaned around him then began to ride him, rubbing her pussy on his lips, tongue, and firm jaw.

Inspired by her show, Dave pressed Kayla's face to the soft carpet and grabbed her hips, lifting them into the air until her knees left the floor. If he was slightly unsteady bracing himself with his bad leg, he made up for it with sheer determination. Still, he only had so many hands to balance with.

Mike paused his fucking long enough to command Joe to help out. "Put his dick in her."

Joe shook his head, trying to clear his mind so he was capable of what they needed. To give them what he could, when they were doing so much for him. He reached out and encircled Dave's fat cock in his fist. If he pumped it a few times, he justified the caresses as getting the other man stiff enough to please his wife.

She looked over her shoulder and shuddered as she saw what he was doing. "Yeah, make him hard, Joe. I can't wait for him to stretch me open. To fuck me deep." Kayla's bright tattoos snaked across her ultra-pale skin, ironic for someone who walked around nude all the time. She was like a living painting. One none of them would ever get tired of looking at.

Or fucking.

Dave growled. "Are you going to help or stare at my wife all day?"

Joe couldn't help jabbing back—it was second nature between them. "You're awfully mouthy for a guy whose nuts are two inches from my fist."

His friend only laughed, his cock bulging impossibly in Joe's hand. "Like you'd do anything to my junk when you know how much your wife adores it."

Morgan didn't help when she moaned at that. Joe didn't blame her; Dave was hung. And he loved sandwiching her between them and giving her the experience Joe was getting off on right then, in between her and Mike.

Knowing when to shut his mouth, Joe tipped Dave's cock forward, notching it against Kayla's pretty, pierced pussy. His own cock pulsed inside Morgan when Dave's tip sank into Kayla, stretching her around his wide shaft. The rings along her labia shifted to let him inside, adding another layer of sensation for them both. Joe guided Dave as he drilled into her, keeping him from slipping out when her tight channel resisted his penetration.

Dave threw his head back and roared as he advanced, each clench of his ass and thrust of his hips fusing him more completely with his wife. "Damn, you're so hot."

"If you ever wore some freaking clothes around here, you might not be so cold," Neil fired off with his smart mouth, making Devon and James chuckle. With the fireplace pumping out heat, none of them would be chilly. That meant nothing compared to the inferno they caused within each other when they shared like this.

It wasn't just about sex. It was about the bonds that joined them into one cohesive unit.

But okay, the sex part was incredible too.

Mike dropped lower over Joe and glided in and out of his ass more fully, with long, even strokes that bottomed him out on each pass. "It's been too long since we did this. Damn, Joe."

He nodded, unable to voice his agreement. But he spread his knees as wide as he could, inviting Mike to use him however he desired. Morgan nipped his lower lip, refocusing his attention on her. He crushed his mouth to hers and feasted, never getting tired of her unique taste and the way they fit together. Her breasts cushioned his chest and the gently rounded stomach she'd had ever since giving birth to their second child made sure he was comfortable as Mike rode him fiercely.

She was soft and warm and so damn strong it made his eyes prickle to think about.

Morgan ran her hands up his sides, making his ass clench around Mike, who cursed.

Kate surrendered a strangled moan, watching Mike fuck as she herself was well pleased by Neil, who ensured she wasn't going to last very long. Especially not when Neil snaked his hand around her waist to rub her clit while he fucked up into her. Neil glanced over to Devon and James, who sixty-nined, and shuddered. Nothing turned him on more than their rapture.

And next to them, Dave matched the pace Mike set as he pumped into Kayla, making her body jewelry jingle as they fucked.

For a while, there was nothing but groans, moans, soft curses, and the wet slap of skin on skin. All of them were steeped in rapture, joined by what they felt when they were experiencing ecstasy simultaneously.

Trapped between Mike and Morgan, Joe felt cocooned in safety. Surrounded by love and lust. Protected from doing something stupid by the two people he could rely on most. And he did need them both. All the rest of the crew, too. What had he been thinking before?

With every plunge of Mike's dick in his ass, which caused him to pin Morgan to the floor, he was reminded of the truth.

They made his life better, in every way. Fuck, especially *this* way.

Joe's cock twitched inside of Morgan's pussy, which began to strangle his shaft. Between her steadily tightening hold and the gravity of Mike's body, he struggled to keep moving.

So Mike did that for him too. He put one hand on Joe's hip and fused them together with a grunt, burying himself as deep as he could go. He locked his cock against Joe's prostate as if he had some kind of stud-finder made for just that sort of thing.

Then he lunged forward, using Joe's body to fuck Morgan.

Her eyes flew open as she realized what they were doing, pleasing her in tandem. Her pink lips formed an O right before her head flew back and her open palms smacked the rug on either side of them. It was the most beautiful thing Joe had ever seen, his wife flying apart, turned on by their primal and honest need for each other and their friends.

He would never get tired of seeing it. Not after fifteen years or a thousand.

And when her pussy wrung his cock, massaging it as she exploded, it was impossible to resist joining her. He tried to warn Mike, but a garbled shout was the only thing that burst from his constricted throat.

"Hell yeah," Mike growled. "Come hard in her. Flood that pussy. Show her how much you love being inside her while I fuck you."

Joe could do that. He let go of everything, worry, fear, and even pleasure. He stopped thinking for one moment of pure bliss and simply felt amazing.

His entire body clenched, then shook as if he was having a seizure. Overwhelmed, every part of him surrendered to the moment and the feelings his loved ones were giving him.

Mike pinned him to Morgan and jerked a few more times, riding Joe through most of his epic orgasm before surrendering himself. But it was the telltale cry from Kate as she came around Neil that tripped Mike's climax, stealing the last of his legendary self-control.

His head snapped up and he stared into his wife's eyes

as he too let go and pumped his own release deep into Joe's ass, filling him with warmth and the proof of their connection, which would never be replaced by anyone else.

Joe lay there and took it. He accepted the reminder and the opportunity to be the vessel for his best friend's pleasure. He let his wife drain his balls dry with the continued milking of her pussy around him.

And so it went, down the line. Like a row of dirty dominoes, each of them fell. Neil clutched Kate to him as he unleashed himself within her. His unmistakable cry of completion reverberated through Devon and James, prodding them to feed their rapture to the other.

And even as Devon swallowed around James's cock, Kayla joined her. The two of them had a special connection that never failed to affect each other. So as Devon came, so did Kayla, rippling along Dave's length until he too conceded defeat. He bellowed. Joe watched his balls draw tight to his body then pulse in time to the seed he shot deep into his wife's body, her pussy still clamping rhythmically around his dick.

Joe's body responded with small aftershocks that echoed through his dick in small spurts that did nothing to slow the pounding of his heart. One of these times it would probably burst when they pushed their bodies to such extremes, and it would be worth it.

He lay in Mike and Morgan's arms, which reached around him to comfort each other as well as him. He gasped for breath until his lungs slowly stopped burning and he could finally, finally relax completely.

They melted into a puddle of limbs and heat.

But when the moment passed, Joe had trouble looking

his friends in the eyes. Because he'd been so close to betraying them and this bond they shared.

What the hell was wrong with him?

When they could move again, Kayla retrieved a basket of towels and other supplies they used to clean themselves up before asking if she could get anyone anything from the buffet. Dave beat her to it, grabbing a plate and serving himself a portion worthy of a man who'd recently come off a month-long fast.

The stillness they'd shared gradually became tender murmurs, and then jokes and laughter filled the room. Everything was as it should be. Except it wasn't.

Mike squeezed Joe's arm after cleaning them up, then asked quietly, "You okay?"

He knew it wasn't the state of his sore ass Mike was concerned about either.

Joe cleared his throat. "Yeah. Sure. Everything's good."

Morgan shot him a concerned glance, even as he caught Devon, James, and Neil doing the same among themselves. Great. Now everyone was going to be up his ass, not quite as literally as Mike had been, until he spilled his guts. And he simply wasn't ready for that.

"Will you be pissed if I want to head out?" Joe asked Morgan, trailing his fingertips along her shoulder. "I'll make you a plate to take home if you're hungry."

"You're not?" she asked.

He shook his head. The only craving he'd had had already been satisfied, and now what he really wanted was somewhere peaceful and quiet to think. Preferably with Morgan by his side. "Nah. Seriously, though, tell me if that's not okay."

"Do I ever get pissed, really?" she asked with a slow,

sensual smile that made him wish he was twenty again and could fuck her right after such a draining exchange.

"Not for long, thankfully. And not as often now that I've learned not to be an idiot around you." Joe grinned, thinking of some of the arguments they'd had when they were younger and hadn't learned to communicate as well as they did now.

Hell, it was like she read his mind when she said, "I don't blame you for wanting to sleep in your own bed after being away for a few weeks. Let me find my clothes and we can go."

"I hope you guys don't mind, but that does sound amazing." Joe scanned the room and his friends, who were crashed out around him.

"As long as I can finish my dinner, I don't care what you do." Dave returned with his plate, throwing a blanket over his lap to keep from dropping anything hot onto his sensitive bits. "But...I am glad you're back."

Joe hoped he could live up to the wary expectation in Dave's gaze, which was mirrored by the rest of his friends. He helped Morgan dress, did the same for himself, and accepted a to-go container from Kayla that he filled with all of Morgan's favorites before leading her to the door.

Her fingers entwined with his as she leaned against his side, half-asleep before they'd even gotten outside. She'd probably doze off in the truck. He sort of relished the idea of carrying her upstairs to their apartment as he had so many times when they were a fresh couple and stayed out partying with the crew too late.

They had history. All of them. And that wouldn't go away ever, no matter what happened from here on out. Maybe that's what his gut had been telling him for a while now.

Joe hesitated with his hand on the doorknob and looked over his shoulder, more confused than ever. "Thanks for...everything."

"You're welcome." Mike smiled and waved. "In fact, come and go from Middletown as much as you want so we can have more parties like this one."

Joe shook his head and flipped off the foreman. "See you at work tomorrow."

Mike chuckled. "We'll bring the kids over when we pick up ours in the morning."

Joe nodded, then ushered Morgan to the truck, tucking her inside before closing the door and rounding the hood to the driver's side. It felt ominous to be taking her and riding away from the rest of the crew in the middle of the night, but also somehow right.

Maybe he'd have to think about what Mike said. Could something like that work? Splitting his time between there and Middletown?

He wasn't sure, but that didn't keep him from spending the entire ride home weighing the pros and cons in his mind.

4

Morgan studied Joe's profile. It was limned by the streetlights they passed under before falling into darkness, then back to light, over and over as they entered town and approached their apartment.

It reminded her of how he'd been acting lately. Off and on. Hot and cold. Bright and dark.

Nothing like his usual, steady, dependable self.

It had her on edge. Tonight had helped, but not as much as she'd hoped. *Damn it.*

She twisted her fingers in the hem of her sweater, annoyed because it didn't escape her how stinking handsome her husband was, even more so now that he had filled out and matured. He only got hotter while she... well, not so much.

Was that what was going on? Was he getting bored of her? Outgrowing her?

Even the crew hadn't seemed to have the same hold over him lately. If she'd learned anything in the years they'd spent together, it was that it was better to talk things out than to let them fester. Especially when they were both relaxed and closer than they'd been in a while after what they'd just done.

Morgan cleared her throat.

"What's up?" Joe asked without having to take his eyes off the road to read her expression. He knew her well enough that he could feel her tension radiating from her.

"Are you going to tell me what's wrong or make me keep imagining the worst-case scenario over here?" she finally blurted, a little less serenely than she had practiced in her mind.

"Oh. Shit." Joe reached over and found her hand, still without looking. He surrounded it in warm reassurance, with a gentle squeeze. "I didn't mean to give off bad vibes. I had an amazing time tonight. Thank you for arranging that. I really...needed it."

"You're welcome." Morgan lifted his hand to her mouth and kissed his knuckles. "I did too. I hadn't realized how wound up we've been and how...off. What really happened in Middletown? Are you okay?"

Joe hesitated, as if debating whether or not to come clean. What the hell?

"We don't keep secrets from each other, remember?" Morgan tried not to raise her voice, but it climbed in pitch if not in volume. He was scaring her, though she was sure he didn't mean to. "Don't ruin my just-fucked peace, please."

He laughed at that. "Sorry. But what I say might do that anyway if I tell you the truth."

Shit, it was worse than she thought. "You're seeing someone?"

Joe swerved to the shoulder and slammed on the

brakes. He stared at her then, his mouth hanging open. "Like who? Who would I want beside you?"

"I don't know." She shrugged, feeling kind of dumb for voicing her darkest fears.

"Cupcake, what could make you think I'd so much as look at anyone else? You're the sweetest woman in the entire world, and the only one I want. You put up with all my shit. The late hours on the crew, the *late hours* with the crew, you know. All of it." Joe unfastened her seatbelt and hauled her into his arms. He kissed her until she could hardly breathe and definitely couldn't argue with his desire. "Maybe I didn't fuck you well enough back at the cabin."

Morgan melted, settling into his fierce embrace. "No, you did. It's just... I don't know. Things have felt a little weird for a while. If it's not that, then what's bugging you?"

"Can we talk about this at home?" he asked with one lingering kiss on her nose.

She nodded and he pulled back onto the street. It took only a minute to park in their usual spot at the rear of her bakery. When she went to open her door, he said, "Stay. I'll come and get you."

"I only had two glasses of wine," she grumbled when he scooped her into his arms.

Morgan held on to their dinner and her purse. She wanted to make sure Joe ate before they finally caved to exhaustion and went to bed. But that might not be for a while yet. It was best that they finish this discussion before the kids were there. They never argued in front of Nathan and Klea, not if they could help it, and never about anything serious.

Then again, they didn't fight much, period.

Joe kicked the door shut, then took her straight to their room before setting her down and taking off her socks and shoes. Then he did the same for himself.

He climbed into bed and dragged her down beside him. Only when they settled in together, in their space, wrapped in each other's arms did he whisper, "I hate being away from my uncle Tom and Eli. And all the rest of the Hot Rods and Hot Rides, to be honest."

"Oh." Morgan craned her neck to look at him directly. "That's it?"

"Uh, yeah." He shrugged. "I mean, isn't that enough? I can't see how I can be in two places at once. So no matter what I do, I'm screwed. Ripped in half. And I don't know how to fix it."

"Joe, I'm sorry you were feeling like that. Why didn't you just tell me?" Morgan rubbed his chest, easing the muscles that had begun to tighten again. It wasn't good for him to be so stressed all the time. Especially not about something he couldn't really change. "We'll make more of an effort to go see them. It's not too far for a long weekend. I'm sure Mike will be flexible with your schedule, and I think Rosie is doing great now that I promoted her to manager. Especially in the summer, we could get out of here every once in a while—"

Joe wasn't as excited as she suddenly felt by the picture she was painting.

So she waited for him to open up to her. "Truth is, cupcake, this place isn't big enough for the four of us anymore. It hasn't been for a while, but we've been making do because it's convenient to the shop and..."

"Sentimental," Morgan supplied softly with a nod. "But you're right. The kids are getting older. They're going to need their own space soon. Privacy as they go through their teenage years."

"So what would you think about moving?" Joe asked.

Morgan's heart spasmed, but it was just a reflexive reaction. She took a second to think about it, then nodded. "I already told you, you're right. We should. I'm going to miss this place. It's filled with so many happy memories, but as long as we're all together, we'll make more in a new place. Maybe I could even have a ginormous kitchen where I could test my recipes and you could have a workshop like you've always wanted. You know, I think there are some lots available out by Dave and Kayla where you could build whatever we like from the ground up."

"We could, yeah. But... As I'm getting older I'm starting to realize that I shouldn't take my family for granted."

"The crew—"

"Not only them." Joe rubbed his eyes, accenting the fine lines that had appeared around them lately. To her, it only made him more attractive, this man he'd grown into as they'd evolved together.

"Just say it, Joe." She put her arms around him and held him tight. "What do you really want? If money or life or anything else holding us back weren't a factor, what would you wish for? Tell me, and we'll work toward it together like we've always done."

"Damn, I love you." He crushed her in his arms before tipping his head down. Instinctively, or maybe through the muscle memory they'd developed over the past fourteen years, they met in a perfect kiss. And when she was breathless, he pulled back long enough to murmur, "I was thinking about a place farther out to start over."

"Like Groveport? Or maybe the Pinebrook area?" Morgan wouldn't love having to make that kind of commute every day, but it was doable if that's what he had in mind. After all, he'd moved in and supported her as they made her dreams a reality. Now maybe it was her turn to support his.

"No. I mean, what about moving to Middletown?" The instant he said it, he froze, as if he couldn't believe he'd proposed it out loud.

"Oh." Morgan blinked, trying not to react too harshly or too hastily. Holy shit. *This* was what he'd been wrestling with. She considered what he was really telling her. That it hurt him to be separated from his uncle Tom, who was getting older, and his cousin, Eli. What right did she have to insist they live apart just so she could enjoy her usual existence without too many disruptions?

But their jobs, their businesses, their family, their friends... No, that wasn't a strong enough word to describe the crew. Their *lovers*. Their lifelong companions.

How would she and Joe make it without them? Would they survive uprooting their entire existence? But if they didn't, would they sacrifice the time he had left with his family in trade for the rest?

Neither was a good option.

Choosing between the crew and his family had to be tearing Joe apart.

She kneaded his chest, trying to comfort him. No matter what they did, they were facing some difficult decisions. As long as they stuck together, they'd figure it out and make it work. So she tried to make him understand that was exactly what they'd do, even if it took her a minute or a month to come around to the direction he'd obviously been heading for a while now. "Can I take some time to process this before we talk about it some more?"

"Yeah. Of course. I didn't mean to drop a bomb like that. It's enough to think of getting a new place. But it just seems with the kids growing up that this is our last chance to make a change before they get to high school and we're locked in for a while longer. I don't want to ruin their friendships and sports and whatever else they get up to, you know? So...if we're going to do it..."

"It would have to be now." Morgan hummed, hating that he was probably right. "Okay. I'm going to really think about it for a little while and then we'll figure it out. Together. We'll make this work, somehow."

When she offered her reassurance, Joe melted into the pillows, looking more exhausted than she'd seen him, even after building an entire first floor of a house in a day with the crew.

"What'd you think?" She got a little annoyed. "That I was going to pitch a fit, or scream at you for being honest about your feelings? Come on, Joe. You should know me better than that by now."

He gathered her into his arms and kissed her sweetly. "I'm sorry, cupcake. I guess I'm just afraid of making a terrible call for us and our family. That's all."

"On our first date, that night in the pumpkin patch, do you remember what you promised me?" she murmured as she stroked his strong jaw.

"That I'd make you come so hard you'd never want to fuck anyone but me and my friends again?" he teased.

She tugged on his scruff.

"Hey!" He laughed.

"I'm being serious." She tried not to let her eyes glaze over as she remembered the moment her life had transformed. The instant all her dreams had begun coming true. Because of Joe. "You said, 'I'm not rich or a genius, but I'll never let you down.' And you know what? You never broke that vow. You've always been there for me. For our family. For us. This time—and every time— we're going to be here for you, too. Never forget that, okay?"

Joe rested his forehead on hers. "You mean everything to me. If this is too much to ask..."

"It's not." Morgan bit her lip as she tried not to concentrate on the sacrifices they'd have to make, even if they only moved to a new home detached from her business instead of all the way to Middletown, and instead thought of how many opportunities the change would bring. "If this is what you need, this is what we'll do. Together. We can work out a detailed plan after we've had some time to mull it over."

"I love you, cupcake." He clutched her close enough that she could feel the impact her faith in him and *them* had on her husband. His pulse pounded in his neck, his eyes were a little too shiny, and...to her surprise...his cock was rock hard against her mound.

"I love you too." She had to make sure he knew it was true. And the best way she knew to prove it was to show him. "Now, let's do something a lot more fun than worrying about the future. The kids are gone and we have all night."

5

———

Relief flooded Joe, making him nearly giddy as he rolled on top of Morgan and crushed his mouth to hers. He intended to be gentle, but hope buoyed his spirits. It got him high on the rush of finally showing her what was in his heart without being instantly shot down.

It shouldn't have shocked him that she was gracious and kind while considering what he had to say, but he'd really thought this time he'd gone too far. Asked too much of her. Maybe moving to Middletown would be over the line, but he didn't doubt what she'd promised for one second. If they worked on the problem together, they'd find a solution eventually.

Joe held Morgan close and stared into her eyes, which were bright even in the soft glow of the bedside lamp. She sighed and said, "I'm serious, I was really lonely without you. Not just being physically far away but emotionally too. Don't do that, please. Whatever happens, I want us to do it together."

"Same." He stole a kiss before sinking more completely onto her.

"I have to admit..." She cleared her throat.

"What?" Joe straightened, having learned through the years when she was saying something important, even if she wasn't shouting to get whatever it was through his sometimes too-thick skull.

"I had a few moments lately where I wondered if it was me, or the kids, and the chaos of our daily lives you were trying to find some escape from on these trips to Middletown without us." Morgan swallowed hard, glancing away from him.

"Shit. No." He rolled to the side, settling into the soft nest of pillows and blankets that she had picked out for them. There was nothing quite like falling into his own bed after having been away. Would it be like that with the crew too? Would what felt exciting—a different environment and new people—morph into a longing for the familiar if he was gone long enough? Would he appreciate the crew even more if he wasn't with them every moment of every day? Or would he realize just how much he'd given up?

Joe was terrified he was going to do something stupid and hurt the people he cared about most, as he'd obviously done to Morgan, at least a little, without even realizing it.

He reached out and cupped her cheek, slowing down to make sure he showed her how precious she was to him. Joe angled her face toward him once more. Without breaking her stare, he promised, "I love you, Morgan. And I'd give my life for you or the kids, you know that. Don't you?"

She nodded, although slower than he'd like. Then she

said, "But duty isn't the same thing as desire. You know Betsy Rae, who comes in on Thursdays to buy a slice of pie for her husband?"

"Uh, yeah." Joe knew most of the regulars who kept Morgan's business thriving. After all, who wouldn't get addicted to the mouth-watering creations she whipped up in the bakery? He'd had to start jogging in addition to his shifts with the crew and their late-night workout sessions in order to keep his six-pack from turning into a keg. Despite his best efforts, he wasn't the young guy Morgan had fallen for either.

Both of them had grown, matured, and hopefully that meant they could work through whatever they were facing now without fear of imploding the life they'd built together.

Maybe. But only if they were open and honest now as he should have been during the months since his unrest began to bubble to the surface.

"Well, she quit buying any two weeks ago." Morgan frowned. "And when I asked her if her husband had lost his appetite or maybe didn't like the seasonal flavors I'd been making, she told me no. That he'd started craving someone younger instead of her and that he could buy his own damn desserts from then on. They're getting a divorce."

"Wow." Joe blinked. He couldn't imagine putting youth above loyalty, a fierce mother for his children, and someone selfless who thought of him first.

But what was his wife trying to say? Could she really think for even one moment that he could ever get tired of her?

"For the record, you're my whole world." Joe shoved the covers to the foot of the bed and slithered downward, intent on worshipping Morgan until she couldn't deny how he felt about her.

"Thanks, but that's not true. There are lots of important things in your life. Our kids, me, your work, the crew, and the rest of your family, like Eli and Uncle Tom. Your honorary nieces and nephews both here and in Middletown..."

Joe refused to let her lump herself in with the rest. "Everything I have is because of you, and I wouldn't throw that away for anything. The other stuff is important, yes, but without you it would fall apart pretty damn quick."

When he kissed a reverent path down her sternum, Morgan murmured, "I'm sorry you've been having to choose between the key things in your life for so long now. And that I didn't realize how much it was costing you..."

She drifted off as her eyes got misty.

Oh no. He wasn't having any of that. Morgan did not cry because of him. Unacceptable. "How could you have if I didn't say anything? Don't take this on yourself. You're an incredible mom, lover, and partner. But you're not psychic. This is about me, Morgan. Not you. Never you."

As he lowered his head to kiss the bottom of her ribs, then her stomach, she tugged him upward and rolled until they were on their sides, staring into each other's eyes. No one on top, no one on bottom. Both equal and every bit as in love as they had been when they first got together.

She met him halfway.

Joe wasn't in a hurry, thanks to their session with the crew. Another thing he had to thank them for—the ability to make slow, sweet love to his wife when they both needed the connection borne of physical intimacy most.

He didn't care if it took all night for them to warm up,

burn, then drift down together into a pile of smoldering ashes. All he wanted was to steep himself in Morgan, bond to her, for as long as possible and to show her that no matter what else changed in their lives, this never would.

Joe sifted her hair through his fingers, then trailed his hand along her neck, over her shoulder, down her arm, across the swell of her hip, and onto her thigh as far as he could reach before beginning upward again. He did it over and over until she practically purred as she kissed him back, feeding her soft sighs and gasps into his parted lips.

The entire time, they locked eyes, hiding nothing from each other.

This was how it was meant to be.

He would be an idiot to do anything that might risk the things he cherished or if he forgot for one moment how lucky he truly was. No one could have everything. He had so much. It should be enough.

"I love you," he told her as he dragged her soft sweater up her body and over her head. His finger traced the edges of her light pink bra. She was so feminine, strong yet subtle. He unwrapped the satin from her as if it was a bow on the best present he'd ever received.

And when she squirmed out of her jeans and kicked them to the foot of the bed, he did the same with her matching panties, this time letting his fingers linger where the material met her even silkier skin. Then he joined her, shedding his own clothes with a lot less fanfare. The urge to be naked with her, exposed in body as much as he was stripped down to his soul, overwhelmed him.

And when he was, he gathered her close so he could feel every bit of her against him.

"You'd think after tonight that I'd be good." Morgan shot him a wry grin.

"You're not?" he asked, trying not to mirror her satisfied expression.

"I mean, I could go for seconds." She glanced away, as if even now it was hard for her to be honest about her desires. Joe tried every day of her life to make her feel safe and loved, but old wounds had left scars. And he planned to keep working to erase them.

"I think we can do better than that. No reason to stop there." He made it his mission right then to make her come apart as often as he could between then and sunrise.

"I'm not Superwoman." She laughed.

"To me you are." Joe stared straight into her eyes so she could see that he meant it.

Then he kissed her once more before reaching over her to her bedside table, where she kept a few essentials, including her favorite purple vibrator. It wasn't some old-fashioned plastic stick. The thing was high-tech, wireless, programmable, made of flexible silicone and it moved in ways that would send him to the ER if he tried to emulate them with his dick.

"If you're not..." she started, but cut off when she glanced down and spied his erection. "Oh."

"I'm saving that for dessert." He kissed her, then snaked lower in bed so he could really see what he was doing. He took her right knee in his hand and raised it so she was spread before him. Thinking of how he'd fucked her and come inside her so hard not that long ago, he groaned.

Then he descended, kissing her pussy even more thoroughly than he had her mouth. He smiled against her when she yelped and gradually melted against him, angling her hips to give him the best access to every part of her.

And when her hands shifted, burying in his hair to hold his face tight to her body, he sucked on her clit. Damn, he could use an extra dick or two. Too bad the rest of the crew was still up at Bare Natural. Morgan's toy would have to do. As advanced as it was, it was still only a tool and not another person. But for right then, it would work.

While he flicked his tongue across Morgan's clit, in the pattern he'd learned she responded to best through the years, he guided the vibrator to her opening. Whether it was because she was undeniably turned on, breathing hard, and squirming as he feasted on her—or because of their earlier encounter—the purple cock slipped right into place against her core. It nudged his chin as he inserted it, aligning it so he could press it into her with a single slow glide.

"Ah," she cried out incoherently, her abdomen tensing in front of his eyes.

"Too much?" He lifted off her just long enough to check.

"No. Not enough." Her pussy hugged the vibrator and her clit stood out, her flesh darkening as she grew more and more aroused. "Turn it on. Please."

Joe smiled up at her. "I should probably be jealous, except I swear I'm going to make you scream louder than this thing when I fuck you next."

Morgan trembled. "I don't doubt that."

Rewarding her honesty, Joe did as she'd requested and flicked the thing on to her preferred mode. It began to squirm in his hand, writhing inside her even as he focused on doing the same to her external anatomy. He hummed when she draped her leg over his shoulder, trapping him in the juncture of her legs, then resumed sucking, licking, and lightly biting her pussy, paying special attention to her clit.

It didn't take very long before Morgan was chanting his name. She arched, her thighs going tight on either side of his neck, so he pulled off, wanting her to savor the moment. When she groaned and reached to bring him back into place, he lunged, rolling her to her back and pinning her wrists to the bed beside her hips.

"Next time we're with the crew, it's going to be your turn. I want you to take them all and let me watch you loving every minute of it." He kissed her mound, then blew across her tight clit, making her shiver. Or maybe it was the gift he was offering her that impacted her so intensely. Because what if it was the last time he could give it to her?

Sure, she was plenty for him, but what was he taking from Morgan if he considered moving? She'd come to expect the attention of as many as five men at a time. Would Joe ever be enough on his own for her?

He blinked, temporarily losing focus.

When Morgan squirmed, he concentrated on bringing her as much pleasure as possible. Whether that was with the crew, or sex toys, or...maybe even the Hot Rods, who knew? Eli had watched them with the crew before, maybe this time he would return the favor and let them, at least, be on the sidelines when the other group was sharing.

Joe would find a way to satisfy his wife, whatever she desired.

And for right that moment, that appeared to be him.

She seemed like she wanted to say something, but the words were lost beneath the mounting pleasure. So instead, he gave her relief. Joe nudged the vibrator up to the next highest setting, then buried his face in her pussy. The thing damn near rattled his teeth out as he sucked and it fucked.

Morgan screamed, a sound he admitted he missed when they had to be quiet making love.

As she shattered in his arms, his cock pulsed. If it hadn't been for the crew and the thorough fucking they'd shared earlier, he probably would have lost it and come all over the sheets.

But now...

Joe rejoined Morgan. He wiped his face on his forearm before resting beside her on the pillows as she basked in pleasure. And when she could take a full breath again, she tipped her head for a kiss. He gave her what she wanted, as he always tried to do. Meanwhile, he blocked out thoughts about what would happen if they were on their own and he couldn't make her happy by himself.

Morgan must have sensed the shift in his mood. In a stern tone she said, "Joe..."

"Huh?" He brushed the hair out of her face, loving the flush that turned her face rosy.

"Don't do that."

"What?"

"Whatever you're thinking or worrying about. It's going to be fine," she promised. "Stay here with me. Tonight it's just us. And this."

And with that, she nudged him to his back and straddled him. She let her soaked pussy slide up and down his length until he was twice as hard as before and bucking upward, eager to be inside her, surrounded by her heat and slickness.

He lunged into a crunch to suck on her breasts,

treating them to the same attention he'd lavished on her pussy. He didn't want them to feel left out. And, fine, he'd always loved her chest. It was a perfect handful for him.

Morgan sighed, then rocked forward while reaching behind herself to stand his dick up. And when she sat back, she took him inside, joining them like they were meant to be.

She moaned and he cursed softly, the ecstasy of that first thrust into her lush body so overwhelming that he couldn't contain it. And when his hands clamped around her hips and his feet planted on the mattress so he could fuck up into her, she settled onto his torso and began to ride.

Her palms laid flat on his chest, kneading his muscles as she used his body to stoke the still-smoldering embers of her passion. It took a good long time, maybe even an hour, of her working over him, savoring the rapture they shared without rushing for the finish before her skin dampened with perspiration and she slipped out of her rhythm.

Both of them groaned. Joe reared up and pressed her to her back at the foot of the bed. He took her hips in his hands and lifted her ass from the mattress so he could slide back inside.

The fat head of his cock reentering her made her shiver all over and goose bumps break out on her arms. Despite having shared him with the crew, and the assistance from her mechanical lover, she was still turned on by this basic lovemaking.

Okay, so there wasn't truly anything simple about it.

Joe understood her body, heart, and soul like no one else and used every shred of that knowledge to light her on fire. Allowing himself to bear down on her with more weight than he would have if she wasn't clawing at his back, silently asking for more, he began to drill into her with ever-quickening strokes. His ass clenched as he concentrated on fast, steady fucking that would take her over the edge.

Both of them. Because once she came, he would too.

There wouldn't be any chance of stopping himself from joining her now.

He grunted as he locked them together as tightly as possible, stared directly into her eyes, and said, "I love you, Morgan."

Her eyelids fluttered and she screamed his name. The clamp of her pussy around his cock was only surpassed by the tightness of her arms and legs squeezing him as they clutched him to her. Joe groaned, then surrendered, allowing his own release to pour from him, flooding her.

He came so hard and so long, emptying his balls into her, that he damn near passed out.

Morgan went completely limp beneath him, her arms and legs falling away as her muscles liquefied. He knew the feeling. After months of escalating tension, they'd wiped it all away and replaced it with this. Absolute peace. Bliss.

Joe wrapped Morgan in his arms and settled her head on their pillows before drawing the comforter up over them. He snuggled up behind her, surrounding her in heat and strength, banding his arm over her waist and between her breasts. Holding her as closely as he could, his heart pounding against her back in time to her own, he dusted the side of her face with butterfly kisses.

"I adore you, Morgan. More each day that we spend together. I swear, nothing about how I've felt lately has anything to do with you. You and the kids are the one thing I've never doubted for a second."

"And the crew?" she asked wearily, utterly worn out.

"I have no fucking idea what to do about them." Joe groaned. "*That's* the problem. How the hell can I choose? It's like deciding if I like my left or right hand better. I need them both. What are we going to do?"

"I don't know, Joe." She put her fingers over his wrist and squeezed, clasping it to her chest. "But whatever it is, we're going to do it together. You, me, the kids. And you know, nothing has to be forever. Our choice can be what's right for right now."

"Hmm." It wasn't really an agreement, but he didn't argue either. And what little resistance was left in his body faded away as he connected with her fully—both physically and emotionally. "You're amazing. You know that, right?"

"You make me feel that way every day." She nestled as close to him as she could get. "You always have, so I need you to know that I'm here for you too."

"Of course you are," he joked, a little of his usual self returning. "Because I'm never letting go of you, cupcake."

"We should get some rest. The kids are coming back at the crack of dawn and they're going to be so excited to see you. They hate being away from you, Joe," Morgan murmured into the still of the very late night. "Almost as much as I do."

"I'm sorry." He nuzzled her neck. "Wherever I go from now on, you're coming with me. Right?"

"Of course."

"Good. Let's start by going to sleep together. See you in my dreams."

Joe didn't know how she managed it, but Morgan fell

asleep with a smile on her face, the same as she had most nights of their lives together. Sure, things were sometimes rocky, but he finally really believed that nothing was ever going to tear them apart. Life had tried and failed over and over.

This time would be no different, even if most everything else they knew changed around them.

6

_____

"Hey, Dad...did you know Jimmy Pickman's parents got him a puppy for his birthday?" Nathan didn't look up at Joe where he was sitting on the couch, his arm slung around Morgan, who had her feet tucked up beside her and was resting against his side while she thumbed through social media to get ideas for new displays.

She glanced up at Joe out of the corner of her eye and shook her head no even as she winced.

"Do you think if I got good grades and do all my chores without you having to tell me and brush my teeth every night, maybe..."

"I wish we could, Nathan." Joe leaned forward and put his hand on his son's shoulder. It was nearly impossible to imagine that in just a few weeks he'd be turning twelve. And before Joe knew it, Nathan would be a teenager, then graduating and moving out on his own. Would he resent Joe for his entire life if he couldn't have the dog bestie he'd been dreaming of for at least half his childhood? Or, for that matter, if he had to share a room with his baby sister when he started going through puberty? "Look at this place. It's hardly big enough for the four of us. Where would we keep a dog?"

"He can live with me and sleep in my bed. Please? Just think about it?" Nathan took a deep breath, then said, "Abby told me that kids who have pets are better at making friends and remembering to take care of stuff because they can practice with their animals."

"She did, did she?" Joe huffed out a laugh under his breath and Morgan buried her face against his shoulder so the kids wouldn't see her grinning. *Jesus*. Abby and Nathan were an adorably conniving duo. They were going to be the death of him and Morgan, and Mike and Kate too.

Joe sighed. They really were going to have to figure something out. He just didn't know what yet. "Buddy, I can't say yes right now. But down the road things might be different. Maybe then—"

"What's that mean?" Klea perked up, turning away from the doll she'd been dressing and redressing in order to level a far-too-adult stare in his direction.

Morgan intervened before Joe could fuck up too bad. Thank God. "Well, honey. Dad and I have been talking. Since you and Nathan are growing up, we're thinking we might need to look for a bigger apartment. A place where you could each have your own room. Maybe even a house that's not on the main road in town, with a yard."

"Where we could have three dogs!" Nathan jumped to his feet and fist pumped.

Joe laughed. "Slow down, Buddy. I don't know about *three*. But one...probably."

"I would have my own room? Really?" Klea tipped her head. She was always so cautious and thoughtful. Kind and quiet. She was definitely Morgan's kid. Shockingly, she was his too. Not that Nathan wasn't his in every way that counted for shit, but biologically...

Klea was a miracle. Both of their kids were. Joe never stopped being thankful for his children.

What was the right thing to do for them? If he and Morgan were going to uproot them, they should do it now, before they got into high school and made those crucial bonds with classmates. The window was closing, and Joe felt like he might be suffocating,

He stood and scooped Klea into his arms. She'd be too big for that soon, but he was going to steal every hug he could before she outgrew his affection. "Yeah, pumpkin. You could have your own room. With a closet for all your dress-up clothes and everything. I could even build you that doll castle we drew up. Would you like that?"

She nodded, but slowly. "As long as it's next to Nathan's room. I don't want to be alone in a big house. I like *our* house."

"Me too." Joe kissed her nose, reminding himself that she was only seven despite how sophisticated she acted most of the time. "But I think it's best for us to think about the future."

"And a puppy!" Nathan reminded him for the forty-thousandth time before flinging his arms around Joe's waist and hugging him tight. From the couch, Morgan snapped a quick photo with her phone, a soft smile making her mouth so sexy he could hardly stand it.

Bedtime!

"Well, why don't we start with the good behavior first and see how things go?" He put his hand on Nathan's back and steered him toward the single bathroom they all shared. "Time to brush your teeth. It's late."

They never were very strict about putting the kids to sleep, wanting to spend as much time as possible with their family. But it was a school night, and getting them up in the morning was a nightmare if they didn't get enough rest.

When Nathan would have whined, Joe leveled a dad-stare at him and he marched into the bathroom with his shoulders only slightly slumped.

"Nice work," Morgan said quietly as Joe carried Klea past her into the bathroom and helped the kids get ready for bed.

He and Morgan had barely tucked them in and kissed them goodnight when Joe's phone buzzed in his pocket. He took it out as he joined Morgan in their room and closed the door behind them. "It's Eli."

Morgan smiled as she climbed into bed and sat with her back resting against the tufted headboard she, Kate, Kayla, and Devon had crafted during one of their ladies' nights a few years ago. He tossed the phone to her then shucked his jeans before joining her.

"Hey, Eli," Morgan answered with a smile. It made him feel so damn good to know that she got along with everyone important in his life. His crew, their wives, and even his extended family. Morgan was perfect in every way. So he had to be sure that any changes they made were right for them both. He owed her that much. "Oh, it's all three of you! A party!"

Joe leaned over so he could see the screen as he drew the covers up to his waist and sat beside Morgan, their legs touching. Eli was sandwiched between his husband, Alanso, and his wife, Sally.

"I'm not sure three of us count for much around here.

It needs to be at least five of us to have a real good time."
Eli grinned despite Sally rolling her eyes.

"Speak for yourself, Cobra," Alanso teased in his thick
Cuban accent. "I have plenty of fun with Sally, no matter
who else is there."

"Ouch." Morgan snorted at their antics. Of course, it
was funny because they all knew it wasn't true. They got
up to some shit individually, Joe was sure, but the three of
them were mated for life. And when they threw in sexy
times with the rest of the Hot Rods, not so different from
nights the crew spent together...well, it was just another
level of amazing.

They were so fortunate. He couldn't forget that. But if
he and Morgan moved out there, where would that leave
them? Would they be welcomed fully into the Hot Rods,
and would either of them really want that? It felt like a
betrayal of the crew to even imagine it, though there had
been times when the two groups had celebrated special
occasions together in the past.

"So what's up?" Joe cleared his throat, shaking himself
from his heavy thoughts. "Miss me? It's only been a couple
of days..."

"I always wish you were here, you know that." Eli
grimaced. "I hate that we're not close, especially at times
like this, when there's things I'd rather tell you in person."

Joe sat upright at his cousin's ultra-serious tone. "Is it
your dad? Is he okay?"

Alanso said something in Spanish, then cracked up,
although Eli didn't. Nor did Joe. The two of them had
dealt with the death of Eli's mom when they were barely
older than Nathan was now. It was something he couldn't
ever forget or stop fearing could happen again. His

kneejerk reaction to unexpected news was dread and panic. Even all these years later.

Maybe that was why he liked giving people fun surprises so much. It helped ease his own anxieties and reinforce the good shit in life. Still, he apparently needed to work more on it.

"No, no. Tom's fine," Eli promised.

"Yeah, probably on round two with Ms. Brown by now. She made him her special cookies tonight. And you know how he likes to show his appreciation..." Sally winked.

Morgan chuckled. "I know from experience that baked goods can have that effect on men."

Joe glanced at her and wondered if Eli would be pissed if they called him back in an hour or two. Because when he locked eyes with Morgan, he knew exactly where her mind had gone—to the chocolate cake the crew had eaten off her way back when in the kitchen just outside this very room. How would they ever leave this place and all their precious memories behind?

Joe licked his lips. Morgan leaned in and kissed him.

"Um, before you two get too carried away..." Eli cleared his throat. "We really do have something important to talk with you about."

"Oh, right. Sorry." Joe shrugged. They would understand. The bond between the threesome on the other end of the video call was every bit as indestructible as the one between him and Morgan. "What did you want to tell us?"

"Well, we sort of need to ask you for some help." Eli took a deep breath. "We have a situation."

"What sort?" Joe narrowed his eyes, taking in the way Alanso was gazing at Sally, with even more honeyed affection than usual. Neither of them seemed too concerned about whatever was eating at Eli. But that was what happened when you were the one in charge. Alpha to the core. Not only in his relationships with his lovers but also as the owner of the Hot Rods car restoration business.

"It seems we're out of space in our apartment above the garage. We need someplace bigger to hold everyone. And we thought, maybe, you might be up for drafting some plans that we could pitch to the rest of the gang." Eli apparently was thinking along the same lines as Joe himself. Except...

"Oh. Yeah. That doesn't seem like such a big deal. You have plenty of room to expand there. What, like...a hundred acres or something?" Joe could already envision a few different approaches. He'd been in construction long enough to have solid ideas and plenty of experience to draw from. Living quarters, a retail operation for the shit ton of merch they could sell now that they were big shots on their reality TV show. Yeah...lots of options.

"I'm gonna need some more room in my pants for expansion soon," Sally said with rolled eyes as she adjusted her jeans, then left her palm low on her stomach.

Joe was still trying to figure out if that was some kind of dick joke when Morgan gasped.

"Hold on." She nearly knocked the phone from Joe's hand as she leaned in closer. "What is this really about? And why are you touching your belly like that? Unless you had a few too many tacos at dinner..."

"This ain't no food baby," Sally said with a slow spreading smile that lit up her usually tough expression. Her face flushed as she looked at Alanso and Eli with a distinctly maternal glow.

"OH MY GOD!" Morgan shrieked loud enough that

Nathan came charging to the door of their room. He knocked—at least the little man had learned that lesson well.

Morgan put her hand over her mouth but bounced up and down as Joe rushed to reassure his son that everything was fine.

"Sorry, buddy." Joe ruffled his hair before turning him toward his room again. "Everything fine. Great, actually. Uncle Eli just told Mom some good news. That's all."

"What was it? Are *they* getting a puppy to keep Buster McHightops company now that he's an old man?"

"Not exactly. It's adult stuff," Joe said. "Thanks for coming to check on us, though. Now go on back to bed."

"But..."

"You have to be responsible to take care of a dog, remember?" Joe used what little leverage he had. He couldn't wait to congratulate his cousin and his spouses. "Night, buddy."

"Night, Dad." Nathan shut the door and the light went out.

Joe rejoined Morgan, hopping onto the bed, not even caring that he was sitting there in his underwear. It's not like the Hot Rods had never seen a half-naked man before. "So you're going to be parents, congratulations! To all three of you."

"Yeah, well... We didn't plan for it to happen. But now that it has, it just...feels right. I'm so fucking happy." Eli put his arm around Alanso, and Sally leaned in to kiss them both.

"And you, Sally? How are you doing?" Morgan had struggled a bit with both of her pregnancies. So she would understand, of course.

"Okay. Honestly, I didn't even realize it for two months.

I'm getting older. I figured maybe my period was on the fritz, but... nope." Sally toyed with the ring in her eyebrow.

"What are you worried about?" Morgan wondered.

"It's kind of late to be doing this and I hope it's safe... for the baby, I mean."

"Have you been to the doctor?" Morgan asked. "I'm sure Nola or Sabra would be more than happy to go with you to talk to an expert or answer whatever questions they can from their own experiences."

The other two Hot Rods women each had children of their own, twin five-year-old boys for Sabra and Holden, and two beautiful girls, who were six and ten, for Nola and Kaige. It would be a bit of an adjustment for the gang to have a baby around again, but with that many helping hands and loving honorary aunts and uncles, Sally would always have help.

"I did go to the doctor, but I was kind of in shock. I didn't ask as many things as I should have." Sally shrugged. "And now, well, we kind of want to tell them in some big, fun way. Like a baby reveal, maybe along with the plans for a new place."

Suddenly it made sense. Of course they needed room to expand if they were going to start a family too. And just like that, Joe felt like he was riding the same exact wavelength as his cousin. Their lives were so parallel right then it made the miles between them twice as long and lonely. His arms ached not being able to hug the guy and slap him on his back.

And now a nephew or niece would be there too... Joe had to be part of their lives.

His stomach cramped as he got more confused than ever.

But one thing he knew for certain.

"We'll help you. Of course," Joe swore. "Let me get my notebook and you can tell me what you think you might like and what the basic requirements are so I can draft a few versions for you to give me feedback on before we do a final mockup."

"Any chance of what we talked about last weekend becoming a reality?" Eli asked coyly. "'Cause I would really like *that*."

"You can speak openly in front of Morgan. Of course she knows how I feel. We haven't reached any decisions yet, but we're weighing our options." Joe reached over and took her hand in his, letting her know that he wasn't going to rip her away from her friends, her business, her home, and everything she'd worked for on a whim. They had a lot more to discuss now, though.

So many things to consider.

"Well, if you want the job—want to oversee the construction, hire a crew here in Middletown, and be in charge of the entire project—the job is yours. You know that right?"

Joe felt shock rip through him. He wasn't a foreman. Mike was.

Going to Middletown had never been about that. About being the boss. He was happy with his role in the crew. But what if...

Maybe it was time for all of them to grow some.

"Thank you." Joe cleared his throat, trying to get himself together. Morgan kissed his cheek and held his hand tight. "This is a lot. I need you to know how excited I am for you. You're going to be great parents. The rest is secondary. No matter what the future looks like for any of us, Morgan and I will always be here to help you out however we can."

"I love you, cuz." Eli took a deep breath, then let it out slowly, as if having Joe's support really meant the world to him. And how could he turn his back on a bond like that? "Okay, we're going to let you go. Give us a call soon and we can talk about the rest—the new place, how the hell to break the news to everyone, and how involved you want to be."

"We will." Morgan grinned and waved at them all. "Congrats again. Love you!"

When they disconnected, Joe sat there, his options weighing heavily on him.

Eli needed him again, maybe more than the crew for right now.

He hoped the guys would understand.

But he accepted that they might not.

7

———

Joe hammered in a series of nails with at least twice as much force as was required. That would have been fine except he got distracted by his thoughts and missed the mark, smashing his thumb in the process. "Shit!"

"Careful there." Mike laughed. "Things break easier these days, old man. Need some glasses to see better?"

"Fuck you." Joe snorted even as he shook the throbbing out of his hand.

"It would be fair enough, since you let me have a turn in you the other night." Mike shot him a not-so-innocent stare. "That doesn't happen very often. Why did you need it?"

"Can't a guy just get off on being fucked every once in a while?" Joe pounded the next nail even harder, relishing the burn in his muscles.

"Sure. But we've been friends long enough for me to know that isn't how you operate." Mike set down his tools and rested his back against the open studs, crossing his arms. "So what's up?"

"I feel guilty as fuck for bailing on Eli and my uncle Tom."

"I noticed you've been spending a lot of time out there lately." Mike cleared his throat. "Your family loves you, Joe. They understand you have obligations. And for the record, when you're out there, you don't need to get worked up like this about not spending time with us. We get it too."

Joe's hammer slipped out of his hand and crashed into the two-by-four in front of him before clattering to the ground. Thank God for steel-toed boots. "What did you say?"

He turned around slowly, surprised to see Mike was dead serious. "It's been obvious for a while now that something's been bugging you. I haven't seen you like this since you and Morgan were trying for kids. I should have pried it out of you sooner."

"I wasn't ready." Joe shrugged. "And honestly, it took a while for everything to come to a head. Maybe not until just this week."

"Because of what happened at the cabin?" Mike wondered.

"Nah, man. Nothing to do with that." Joe joked because it was easier than telling Mike straight up that their physical connection had been what kept him sane, not what drove him over the edge. "Your cock is big, but it's not Dave-sized or anything."

"Gee, thanks." Mike shook his head. "So what happened?"

"You can't say anything..." Joe leveled a stare at Mike. He might be the foreman, but they were friends first.

"I don't like keeping secrets around here, you know that."

"Yeah, except it's not really my news to spill. I need you to understand, though." He and Morgan hadn't had a chance to hash out the repercussions of their recent discussion, but the facts were the facts. What they did about them... Well, maybe Mike could help him think more clearly about that.

"This sounds serious." Mike's eyes narrowed. "Is everyone okay?"

"Yeah, yeah. Sorry." Joe lowered his voice, although no one else could hear over the din of power tools running somewhere else in the house they were flipping. "Sally's pregnant."

"Sally? Holy shit. That's great! Congratulations, Uncle." Mike crossed the floor between them to smack Joe's back in a genuine man-hug. Of course he meant it. He hadn't thought through the ramifications yet.

But it didn't take him long. He held Joe out at arm's length. "Oh. That's not going to help your homesickness, is it?"

"This is home. The crew is home."

"Maybe it can be more than one place," Mike said quietly. "There's a part of you there with them already, and this is only going to make it grow. As it should. Your kids should know their cousin. It's a special bond, as you know considering how tight you are with Eli."

And there it was. The thing that Joe had been mulling over incessantly since the good news had sunk in. "There's more."

Mike's eyebrows climbed. "How much more?"

"They're out of space at the garage. Eli wants me to draft up some plans for an expansion. A new house, a massive one, to fit them all with room to grow. And maybe some merch areas too." Joe brushed sawdust from his jeans, which was pretty futile given the state of his work clothes. But it was better than looking Mike in the eye when he said, "They asked me if I want to manage the project. Hire guys and stay on long term to—"

"Become the foreman of your own crew." Mike didn't say anything else for a few seconds. His mouth opened and then closed. And when Joe braced himself for scorn or fury, Mike instead shoved out his hand. Not in a fist, but for a shake.

"Double congrats then. You deserve this opportunity." When Joe didn't clasp Mike's hand right away, the other guy wrapped his fingers around Joe's and shook for him.

"It's not a done deal," Joe insisted. He never would have accepted a new position without talking to Mike and the rest of the Powertools first. He might be a traitor, but he wasn't an asshole.

"Why not?" Mike tipped his head. "Not that I'm kicking you out or anything, but I can see that you want it. That you'd love to spend more time with your family. I know we've done jobs for them before but that was small stuff we could knock out in a week or two. We won't be able to leave our projects here for that long, not all of us. But you can."

"You know I think of you guys as family too, right?" The last thing he wanted was for his feelings to be misconstrued or for his ambition to injure his partners. "This has been killing me. I can't sleep. I can't eat. Hell, Morgan thought I wasn't into her because I didn't even want to fuck as much."

"I noticed that too." Mike's jaw clenched.

Damn it, Joe was screwing this up too. And it was only going to get worse if he ditched the crew. How could they ever believe how agonized he was about it? "There's other factors. We have to move anyway…"

"You do? Why?" Mike stepped back and crossed his arms. Uh oh. This was taking a turn for the worse.

"Because our place is tiny and the kids aren't anymore. Nathan wants a puppy and I can't even give him that where we're at now. They're going to be teenagers in a minute and they need their own space. Pretty soon they're going to be in high school, a terrible time to uproot them. So we need to act now." His worries came pouring out in a flood.

Instead of arguing, Mike was silent for longer than Joe was entirely comfortable with. Finally, he nodded. "I see where you're coming from. So what are you going to do?"

"I don't know yet. Morgan and I are still trying to figure that out."

"Well, you know I've always got your back." Mike could have made it easier on him if he'd acted like a jerk. But no, he did what any person who loved another did. He prepared to let them go when needed, no matter how bad it hurt.

Which was exactly why Joe couldn't find the right way to move forward. How could he when he regretted what he was leaving behind with every step he took toward the future?

"How the fuck am I going to make this work?" Joe asked, staring up at the ceiling as if for divine guidance.

"Look, next weekend is a holiday. Why don't you drive out there? Celebrate with Eli, Alanso, Sally, and Tom. Talk about this shit in person. This isn't the kind of stuff you should do over the phone. Hell, take Morgan with you this time. Kate and I will watch the kids. We'll take them camping with us. Abby and Landry will love it."

Neither of them said what they were thinking, that it might be one of the last times their kids got to hang out together for a while, so they should make the most of it.

That plan sounded good to Joe too. Maybe with some time alone, he and Morgan could hash things out. With fresh eyes maybe she could see all the possibilities he envisioned when he visited Middletown.

"I'm not finding a reason to say no here." Joe scrubbed his hand through his hair. "Let me run it by Morgan, but I think we'll probably take you up on that if you're sure."

"Of course I am. About all of it." Mike clasped Joe's forearm for a moment, then stepped back slowly. "You deserve the best. And if they can give you that, you should be willing to hear their offer with an open heart and an open mind."

"Thanks, Mike." Joe snatched his hammer off the ground and shoved it into the belt at his waist. "I knew you'd understand. And that only makes this ten times as hard."

"Just the way we like things around here. Big and hard." Mike cracked up as he turned back to their project. Except this time it might have been him hammering the nails with a little too much force.

8

———

"This place is gorgeous." Morgan's breathy gasp echoed as Joe let her into the home they'd rented for the weekend. The entryway opened to a wide staircase.

"Upstairs there are four bedrooms. Down here there's the kitchen, a living room, a big dining room where you could have dinner parties without crashing at someone else's place, and there's even a sunroom off the back." Joe figured it was exactly the sort of home they'd choose for themselves if they built from the ground up. Crown molding everywhere, upgraded lighting fixtures, high-quality finishes he'd love to install in a place he got to stay with his family. It would be a chance for him to put his craft to the best possible use, to make a home for his family. And here, in Middletown, they could easily afford both the land and the construction costs on a place like this.

If they moved, this could be their future.

"I'm not going to lie. I could get used to this." Morgan walked to the rear of the home and peered out the expansive windows. It had lovely landscaping, a yard that stretched forever, and enough bathrooms that each of the four of them could take a shower separately but simultaneously.

When she turned and spied the kitchen, her eyes nearly popped out of her head. She dragged her fingertips over the stainless steel appliances so lovingly he tried not to be jealous. Then she admired a giant marble-topped island and even an appliance garage that hid a stand mixer along with other doodads.

"You don't mind that we're not staying at Hot Rods?" Morgan asked Joe while testing out the high-arched faucet you could easily put a giant pot under.

"We're right down the street. That's close enough. Besides, Eli wasn't joking. There really isn't room for them, never mind us. I'm not going to make you bunk on the couch like we're teenagers bumming our way through trade school again." Joe had taken the drive out there to reflect on how far he'd come in the past twenty-five years, but also to focus on the road ahead, and where it could take them if they were courageous enough to keep traveling onward together.

"I don't know, that sounds kind of fun." Morgan smiled at him over her shoulder. "But this is...incredible."

"The owner told me she has a monthly rate and she just had a cancellation for the whole summer." Joe shook his head. "Wouldn't that be something?"

"We'd never be able to squish ourselves back in our apartment after spending that much time in a home like this." Morgan sighed. "I didn't realize we'd outgrown that place, but you're right. We have. No matter what, we're not staying there."

Joe put his hand on her shoulder and kissed the side

of her neck from behind her. "There's no rush. If you're not ready yet…"

"I am." She clasped his hand. "It's scary, but also exciting. Don't take my mixed emotions as regret. It's not that. It might just take a bit of getting used to."

"Fair enough." Joe hugged her tight to his chest.

"I think it scares me most because I can so easily picture us here," she whispered. "What do you think would happen if we moved? Would we be part of the Hot Rods gang like we are the Powertools?"

"Are you asking if we'd share with them?" Joe's arms dropped to his sides and he took a step back. He'd thought about it but it was another thing to hear it from Morgan. Is that what he wanted? They'd definitely gone as far as watching before. But joining in? He wasn't sure about that. Would it be awkward or awesome? Would it take away from the special connection they had with the crew?

Morgan wandered to the other side of the kitchen, peeking into the fancy refrigerator with its multiple-setting icemaker and modern freezer configuration. He knew she was trying to occupy herself instead of staring him down as he mulled over her question. To give him time to really think about what she was asking. If that's what she needed…

It had always been her fantasy to have more than one guy at a time, and heaven knew he'd gotten off on watching her blow his friends' minds. "I'm not ruling anything out. I have no idea what the Hot Rods would think of that, but if you were interested, I'd talk to Eli about it."

Morgan shrugged as if it had been an offhand remark. Had it? Or was she simply shy about proposing that they swing with another group of friends than the ones they'd fooled around with for years? He couldn't tell, but either way, he didn't want to scare her off of sharing her hopes and desires with him.

While he was trying to figure out the right thing to say, she turned sideways and studied her distorted reflection in the gleaming, spotless refrigerator door before cupping her breasts, pushing them halfway to her neck. "Maybe I should get a boob job. What do you think?"

He cracked up.

Until he realized she wasn't joking.

"Wait. What?" He crossed to her and replaced her hands with his own. "I think your chest is one of your sexiest features."

"I used to think that too." She sighed, leaning against him. "But kids and gravity, you know? I'm forty now. Things are only going to keep going downhill, literally, from here..."

"I love you exactly the way you are."

"That's not the same thing as being attracted to me." She closed her eyes as if she didn't adore what she saw, like he did. "Especially if we're going to consider getting naked in front of new people."

"Cupcake, come on." He nuzzled her neck and let her feel exactly what it did to him to have her this close and warm in his arms. "Do you really think I don't want you?"

"Okay, fine. You do. Still, the Hot Rods are younger than us."

"Not by much. And second, they've had their own share of kids and...well...life. No one's perfect. That's not what we do is about." Joe kissed her until she loosened up some in his arms.

Morgan opened her eyes and pulled back. "I know. I

do. It's been a long time since I had to worry about what someone thought of me in that way. I guess I took for granted what it meant to be secure in the knowledge that you and the rest of the crew wanted me."

"If there's someone who's not into you then, fuck 'em. I can't help if they don't know perfection when they see it, but I certainly wouldn't be offering to share my wife with anybody who didn't appreciate her as much as I do." Joe felt his hackles rise at even the thought. No matter what, he'd protect Morgan.

"Yeah, you're probably right. It's a dumb idea," Morgan said as she wandered off to explore the second story of the house. That didn't keep her from looking over her shoulder as if appraising her perfect ass in the hallway mirror before she climbed the stairs. Her hand rested lightly on the polished wooden railing as she ascended.

"From here, I can tell you there's nothing wrong with this view." He swatted her butt as he trailed her up to the master bedroom.

She smiled at him and took his hand while they admired the spacious master suite, which their entire apartment could have fit in. And when she spotted the bright white soaking tub on a platform with a breathtaking view of the backyard and the onion fields beyond, she went still.

"Hey, Morgan. Seriously, though." Joe put his hands on her hips as they stood there and looked at what could be their destiny. "It's your body and I want you to be comfortable in it. If a tune-up is what you want to feel good, do it. Just know that you don't ever have to change anything for me to love you—or be attracted to you. I already do and always will."

"Thanks," Morgan murmured before linking her

fingers with his and leading him to the giant four-poster bed in the other room. She sank to her knees on the plush carpet in front of him and unbuttoned his pants.

"What are you doing down there?" He probably should object, but when her fingers reached into the fly of his jeans and took out his now-hard cock, he wasn't about to stop her from getting him ready to prove what he'd sworn to her.

"Showing you how much I'm still attracted to you too." Morgan smiled up at him before kissing the head of his dick sweetly. Then she opened her mouth and took him inside slowly and very deliberately.

Her fingers tightened on the back of his thighs as she braced herself, then went deeper, laving the underside of his shaft with her flattened tongue.

"Damn, Morgan." Joe speared his fingers into her hair. He'd fuck her so good for making him wild with desire. In just a few more minutes. He closed his eyes and savored the sensation of her pleasing him, the way only she knew how.

Her fingers teased his balls as she sucked on him, guaranteeing they were going to christen the beautiful bed behind her. When he couldn't bear standing there without her in his arms a moment longer, he put his hands on either side of her ribs and lifted her up, her mouth leaving his hard-on with a wet sound that did nothing to improve his self-control.

He kissed her, pausing only long enough to pull off first her shirt, then her bra. And when he grabbed his own T-shirt, she slipped out of her pants and yanked his down. Joe kicked them off then practically tackled her onto the bed.

They rolled, laughing until he landed on top of her. Then it was time to be serious.

He rubbed himself across her, his dick nudging her mound as he reveled in the softness of her body against his. Just as he took his cock in hand to fit it to her and slide inside, his phone started ringing.

"Ignore that," she huffed as she clutched his shoulders and drew him to her. But when it rang again, she stopped. "Wait. What if it's the kids?"

Joe groaned. He lunged for his jeans and fished out his phone. It was Eli. Joe unlocked it with an irritated, "Is this important?"

"You're not fooling around, are you?" Eli asked with a knowing laugh. "Keep your dick in your pants until tonight."

"Too late," Joe grumbled. "Can I call you back?"

"No need. Just do what you gotta do and get your ass over here. Ms. Brown made her famous apple pie and it smells so good. We can't eat without the guests of honor."

Joe knew there was more to it than that. They were waiting for him and Morgan to tell the rest of the Hot Rods their good news. "I'm pretty sure Sally is about to rightfully take that place."

He couldn't wait to see the looks on their friends' faces when the trio announced their special news. Still, there was no way he was leaving his wife wanting, her flushed face and dilated eyes telling him exactly what she needed right then. "Give us fifteen minutes and we'll be there."

They were right down the road, could make it in under five.

Joe could do a lot with the other ten.

Morgan laughed and grabbed the phone from him. "See you soon enough, Eli. Gotta go. Love you. Bye."

She hung up, then tossed it onto the side table before rolling to her stomach and getting to her knees. She put her ass in the air and her face on the fluffy pillow, then looked back at Joe coyly. "You going to finish what you started?"

"Hell yes." He smacked her ass and got to work.

Joe braced one hand on her hip as he plunged into her body, making her cry out his name as he bottomed out in her with a single stroke. And when he was fit to her as tightly as possible, he reached around with the other to rub her clit as he began to fuck.

After a minute or two, she began to moan each time his balls tapped her clit next to his finger, so he leaned forward, his teeth sinking into her shoulder. He'd never felt as proud or possessive of her as he did right then. She was his partner in every way, and as long as they both remembered that, everything else would work out.

It would be fine. Better than.

Joe pumped into her harder and faster as the possibilities rushed through him. Her pussy clamped down on his dick, trying to stifle his movement, but he pushed through, riding her until she couldn't help but fall apart in his embrace.

And when she did, screaming, he joined her, pouring his release into her as deeply as he could.

Surrounded by her heat and strength, he gave her everything he had, as he always would.

9

Morgan couldn't say why she was nervous as they walked around the back of the Hot Rods garage, past Tom and Ms. Brown's house to the picnic shelter and barbecue area where all the gang's family functions took place, at least in good weather. It was a glorious day, the kickoff of summer, and no matter what else happened, they were about to deliver some very good news in the form of one very special cake she'd baked.

Despite the fast, hard orgasm Joe had given her, she couldn't seem to shake her nerves.

"They're going to love it, cupcake," Joe promised her. He didn't hold her hand because he cradled her creation as if it was as precious and fragile as the tiny baby it was going to announce.

"I think they will." She smiled up at him. But would the rest of the gang take to Eli's suggestions?

Because all of a sudden, she was starting to care what they thought and whether or not it affected their chances of making some sort of move.

Huh.

"Joe!" Uncle Tom spotted them first, striding over with a giant, welcoming grin on his face. Morgan intercepted him for a warm and very reassuring hug as Joe set the cake, covered in an opaque black dome, at the far back of the dessert table. "How's my favorite nephew's wife today?"

"Uncle Tom, I'm your only nephew," Joe snorted as he took up where Morgan had left off.

"True enough, but you'd be my favorite even if I had a dozen."

"Sure, sure." Joe slung one arm around Morgan's shoulder and tucked her against his side. She loved how they fit together and how natural it was after all the years they'd been a couple.

"We're great, Uncle Tom," Morgan promised. "So happy to be here today."

"And we're glad to have you. I have to admit I was surprised to hear Joe was coming back so soon. But not sad about it. Not at all." Uncle Tom shot Joe a decidedly loaded gaze. "Any reason for the trip?"

"If you're asking if I've talked to Morgan about what you and I discussed last time I was up here, yeah, I have." Joe looked at her and smiled. To see the joy and relief radiating from him reassured her they were making good decisions.

"And?" Tom asked Morgan this time.

"We'll see." She didn't want to give too much away. Especially not when Ms. Brown joined him. The two might not have been together as long as she and Joe, but they were every bit as right for each other.

"What's all this whispering about?" Ms. Brown wondered, her eyes a bit too keen for comfort.

"Nothing yet," Joe deflected. "But maybe something soon."

"Hmm." Ms. Brown didn't pry right then, but she wouldn't let it go for long. "Well, whatever it is, I hope it works out for the best for you both. And until then, let's eat!"

When she clapped her hands for attention, everyone turned to look.

Morgan found herself and Joe surrounded by the seven mechanics and their families that made up Hot Rods. In addition, their Hot Rides cohorts swarmed them until they were surrounded by friends and family. She couldn't resist smiling when she received hug after hug, and so did her husband.

They might not have the crew, but Joe was right—they had a lot of family here.

Sally wormed her way through the throng so Morgan squeezed her tight. "How are you doing?"

"Perfect." She beamed. "And you? The cake?"

"It's all set. Just like we talked about." Morgan high-fived the woman, who was responsible for turning the cars at Hot Rods restoration into amazing works of mobile art with her spectacular paint jobs.

"Thank you so much." Sally knuckled a tear from the corner of her eye before anyone else could detect it. That would raise the alarm for sure. Sally wasn't a crier. She whispered conspiratorially, "Fucking hormones."

"Don't worry, it only gets worse." Morgan laughed at Sally's scowl. "But it's so worth it. Congratulations."

Sally nodded, then drew Morgan with her to take their seats. Joe and Eli talked during the entire meal they shared, while Alanso split his time between joking with the guys and casual discussions with her and Sally.

Around the table, all the couples and their kids mixed, mingled, and enjoyed each other's company.

Morgan imagined Nathan and Klea sitting at the kids' table playing with their friends. It wasn't hard to do. As much as they were members of the Powertools crew, part of them also belonged here. No wonder Joe had been struggling with the halves of himself for so long.

As the clink of forks lessened and the talking grew louder, Morgan excused herself. She had to pee and didn't want to risk waiting too long and missing the big moment. She emerged from the restrooms the Hot Rods had gotten Powertools to add to their facilities a couple years back on one of their quick trips and nearly ran smack into Kyra, the drummer for Kason Cox's band, who happened to be dating both the Hot Rides salvage man, Ollie, and a key member of Kason's security team, Van.

That lucky bitch. She had two sexy men in her bed every night. Even if that bed was awfully cozy, since the three of them—and Ollie's pet hedgehog Mr. Prickles— lived in a campervan that allowed them to tour and tag along on Ollie's junkyard runs for the Hot Rides motorcycle shop.

"Oops!" Morgan laughed a bit as she tried to dodge Kyra, but the other woman grabbed her arm instead.

"Sorry, I was sort of stalking you." Kyra winced. "Bad choice of words. Sorry again."

The woman had some trouble with an overzealous fan not too long ago. But even so, she was normally one of the most badass women Morgan knew. So what was with the apologies?

"Why are you so nervous?" Morgan looked around. "That guy who was bugging you..."

"Oh. Shit. No. Nothing like that." Kyra's smile was far

too big and bright for there to be something serious going on.

"What's up?" Morgan asked, her head tipped as she waited patiently for Kyra to confess.

"I was wondering if you would talk to Joe for me."

"Talk to me about what? I don't bite, you know." Joe grinned as he joined them, making Kyra jump. "Not unless I'm asked nicely."

Morgan swiped at him playfully. "Come on, she's being serious."

"You okay?" Joe asked.

"Very." Kyra nodded, waving Ollie and Van over to huddle up with them.

The two guys flanked her, beaming just as she was. "Did you tell them?"

"What is it?" Morgan was normally patient, but even she had her limits. "You're killing me!"

"Well, we're sort of...going to make things official. I mean, as official as can be." Kyra held out her hands and clasped one of each of her guys', who smiled at each other. *Damn, girl.*

"That's amazing!" Morgan wondered how Middletown could contain the endless happy shit that went on around there. Of course, each of the couples, or more, who lived there now had gone through rough times to find their happily-ever-afters. They deserved the best the world had to give. "Congratulations!"

"But...ummm... we were wondering..." Kyra looked to Ollie then.

He picked up where she got stuck. Asking favors wasn't easy for any of them even now. "Would you be interested in helping us build a place of our own up on the Hot Rides land? If I talk to Gavyn about it and maybe buy a piece or something. We're looking for a space a little bigger than a tiny house, or our van. Because..."

"We want to start a family," Van blurted. "Like...the sooner the better. And we need more room. And someplace stable. And, well, we thought you would be the perfect person for the project. I mean, I know you already have a job but...maybe we could figure something out?"

Joe narrowed his eyes. "Have you been talking to Eli?"

"Um, no," Kyra said. "I didn't know we needed your cousin's permission to get married and have a baby or five."

"*Five*?" Ollie gulped.

Kyra patted his hand but didn't look away from Joe. "Wait... Why?"

Morgan smacked her husband in the gut with the back of her hand, then said, "No reason. None at all. Um, I think we can help you out, but maybe we better think about it a little."

"Oh yeah. Of course." Van did a shit job at hiding his disappointment. Morgan hugged him, afraid to say another word and ruin Eli, Alanso, and Sally's surprise. How the hell her husband constantly pulled them off boggled her mind. This was a lot of effort!

Just then, two boys about five years old—mirror images of each other—burst from behind the bathroom. Their mops of shaggy brown hair made them look exactly like their dad, Holden. Before Morgan could so much as say hello to them, they sprinted toward the pavilion and started shouting. "Mommy, Mommy! Did you know Van, Ollie, and Kyra are getting married? Do you think Mr. Prickles going to be the ring bearer? Isn't that so cool how we found out first? We told you we would make good super-spies!"

Everyone stopped and turned as one to stare at the five of them.

Kyra waved awkwardly at the crowd. Together, they shuffled toward the gathering as she confirmed. "Um, yep, it's true. Surprise!"

Morgan winced as she saw Sally look to Eli and then Alanso and shake her head. She didn't want to step on their friends' toes with her own major announcement.

"Oh shit," Joe muttered beneath his breath. Morgan took his hand and squeezed it tight.

Everyone crushed the trio in a round of hugs and well wishes. Doubly so when it came to Sally, who hugged her friend and rocked her back and forth while squeezing her tight.

Morgan could practically see the love swirling around everyone there. Just like in the crew, they supported each other and rooted each other on. When you had a support system like that, how could you not make your dreams come true?

It was probably in that instant that she realized she was fully onboard with Joe's plan. Now she just needed the right time to tell him so.

"Well, the best way to celebrate news like this is with dessert!" proclaimed Quinn, Roman's little brother, who was also the manager of the Hot Rides garage.

Things happened in slow motion after that.

Quinn reached for the special cake Morgan had baked and whipped the lid off as Sally and Morgan dove toward it, shouting, "No!"

But it was too late.

It was revealed to everyone in all its multi-tiered, sprinkled and obviously birthday-candled glory. They outlined the zero she'd made out of mango coulis on top.

"Uh. What's this about?" Quinn scanned the gathering as if mentally calculating. "Did I forget someone's special day?"

Morgan looked to Sally and said, "Maybe I grabbed the wrong cake out of the case?"

"That's a load of crap if I ever heard one." Ms. Brown had had enough. "You two have been acting suspicious since you got here. What are you up to? What is going on?" She wagged her finger between Morgan and Sally, clearly having the best bullshit-meter in all of the city. Morgan felt bad for her daughters, Nola and Amber, who were also there with their families—one a Hot Rods' wife and the other married to Gavyn, who owned the Hot Rides empire. They probably hadn't been able to get away with a damn thing as teenagers.

"You might as well just tell her," Nola said with a shrug. "She never gives up. She's like Buster McHightops with a bone."

The Hot Rods' old dog rolled over as if telling them to surrender.

"Okay, fine!" Sally threw up her hands. "I'm sorry, Kyra. I didn't mean to steal your thunder. I didn't know, I swear."

"Of course you didn't." Kyra took her hand, then snorted. "We should have known better than to try to talk about anything stealthy around here. What's this cake about and can I have some? It looks incredible, and so happy. And...significant."

Morgan stood up straighter at that. Mission accomplished.

"It's a pre-birthday party. About six months early." Sally sent a wobbly smile to Alanso and Eli, who each put a hand on her shoulders.

"Are you saying...?" Tom tried to keep his shit together, but Morgan could feel him practically vibrating with pent-up energy.

"Yeah, Pops." Eli looked around at all their family gathered and said, "We're having a baby."

For the second time that day, everyone whooped and cheered and hugged and teased. Morgan melted as she was caught up in the center of the whirlpool of jubilation. It was powerful and profound and moved her in ways she couldn't explain.

She turned to Joe and pulled him down to her for a warm, slow kiss. The pure delight in his gaze as he brushed his lips over hers told her everything she needed to know. They could be happy here.

They were so lost in each other, Morgan didn't realize Alanso was explaining their plans to expand their living quarters and the offer they'd extended to Joe until people started slapping him on the back and jarring her in the process.

"So be on your best behavior today because Joe and Morgan are here to feel things out and make up their minds about whether they can stand us for longer than their usual visit." Alanso ruffled Joe's hair, then embraced both him and Morgan, laying a loud, smacking kiss on her cheek. "*Gracias*. The cake is beautiful and having you both here, especially today, means so much to Eli. To us all."

Morgan sniffled, suddenly overcome with emotion.

And that was even before Tom descended to crush first Eli and Alanso and Sally and then Joe and Morgan in big bear hugs that only he could give.

Before he'd even finished clutching them, his warm stare saying everything he didn't have words for, Morgan's cake had been cut and was being enjoyed by everyone.

"I'm so jealous!" Devra, Quinn's wife, forked a bite into her mouth and closed her eyes on a hum as she neared Morgan. "How did you get this to be so moist? And the flavor! Is that lemon raspberry? A hint of mint? It looks like candy but tastes like five stars."

Morgan jumped up and down, then squished Devra to her for saying so. The restaurateur had high standards when it came to food and she'd nailed the flavor profile exactly. "That means so much coming from you."

"You know... If Joe is going to be here, working on some projects for the gang, maybe you and I could collaborate on stuff for the restaurant. I have a whole area up front I've been toying with merchandising for carryout products. I would put in a bakery case in a second if you were there to fill it for me." Devra eyed her slyly over another forkful of cake.

Morgan looked to Joe, but he simply shrugged and left her to discuss her business with Devra, who ran her own as well. He had always trusted her to do that and so she knew, deep down, that she needed to give him the same respect. If he wanted this job, she was going to stand behind him and create new opportunities for herself while she was at it.

It wasn't until much later, as they were in the car headed back to their house—rather, the place they'd rented, even if it already felt like it could be home—that Joe completed the final piece of the puzzle for her.

"Did you see the pups?" he asked.

"Pups?" She shook her head as she looked over at him.

"Sorry, you were talking with Devra and I didn't want to interrupt, but yeah, I guess Buster McHightops found them abandoned somewhere, out in the woods. He carried them back to Hot Rods."

"Kind of like Tom did for the mechanics." There was some kind of poetic resonance with that. Each of the Hot Rods had been adopted by Tom after passing through the youth shelter his wife had founded before her tragic, early death.

"And sort of like Bryce did for Buster when he rescued him from that scrap metal behind the shop." Joe nodded, never taking his eyes from the road, brightly illuminated by his headlights, guiding the way for them. "I'll show them to you tomorrow when we go back over there. There's this one. It's super playful and really sweet. I was thinking...if things work out...it might be old enough for Nathan by summertime."

Morgan's heart swelled. After everything they'd done and shared that day, she knew that nothing would mean more to Joe than to surprise their son with the wiggling bundle of cuteness he'd dreamed of for so long. There was no chance she'd say no to that regardless of what else they decided to do.

"God, I love you," Morgan whispered, her hand sliding over his on the seat between them. "Every time I think it's not possible to love you more, you do something and prove me wrong again."

He turned into the driveway and parked at the foot of the stone path that led up to their house before coming to help her out as he always did. "And even still, you can't possibly love me as much as I love you, cupcake."

"It was really good to see you smile so much today." Morgan hugged Joe tight. "I'm glad you had such a good time."

"It's going to be an even better night," Joe promised. And she believed him. "But what about you? What did you think?"

They strolled up the path together, hand in hand.

"You should accept their offer." Morgan paused and made sure to look him straight in the eye when she spoke, so he could see she really meant it.

"Seriously?" He seemed to stop breathing.

"Yes." Morgan filled her lungs for them both then said, calmly, "The kids will be done with school in six weeks. That should give you time to put out a call for crewmen, finalize your designs, and file for permits. I'll talk to Rosie and see if she feels comfortable running Sweet Treats for three months. We'll come out here for the summer, rent this house, build Eli's place, work on Kyra's project, collaborate with Devra, and see if this is really what we want. Get a sense of how the kids might adjust. And give them the puppy they've been asking for forever."

Joe whooped and twirled Morgan around. "You're a genius. Yes. That sounds perfect. It feels right. Doesn't it?"

"I know there will be sacrifices..." Morgan swallowed hard as she thought of being so far away from Kate, her best friend since they were kids, and the rest of the crew.

"Big ones." Joe grew somber.

"But, yes." Morgan nodded. "It feels right. I can't wait to see what you do for the Hot Rods. Plus Devra and I have so many ideas that could lead to new prospects for me too. It's—"

"Exciting!" Joe laughed as he unlocked the door then walked inside backward, drawing her first up the stairs and then toward the bed.

They hadn't had this kind of energy zinging between them since the early days when she'd been fighting to make her shop a success and they'd tried so hard to start a family. Maybe they'd gotten too comfortable in their current lives. Because now that a challenge was laid out before her too, he was right. It was exhilarating to contemplate leveling up again.

He continued, "And scary as fuck. But as long as we're together, everything will be perfect. You were right about that."

Morgan clung to Joe as they toppled, bouncing together on the mattress. They both grinned before they came together, making out as enthusiastically as they had when they'd first met and gotten hooked on the taste of each other.

It was a beginning, and maybe also an end. Until right then she hadn't realized it was possible to mourn and be overjoyed at the same time. It was bizarre and confusing, but also made her feel alive in a way she hadn't in a while.

Joe only enhanced that pleasure when he lived up to his promise to make love to her all night long. Energized and reinvigorated, it seemed like each epic orgasm he gave her topped the last. Just like in life. Every time they survived one of these twists fate threw at them, they ended up closer together.

And this time would be no exception.

10

"You've been grinning like an idiot since you got back from Middletown." Mike might have acted casual when he said it, but his shoulders were damn near hiked to his ears as he marked some cuts on the back of the tile they were installing in their latest flip project.

"Some alone time with Morgan is always a good thing." That was part of it. But not all of it. Joe finally felt like they were both on the same page. It was the Powertools he was still hiding from.

"When are you going to tell the rest of the crew what's going on?" Mike asked.

"The time never seems right." Joe shrugged, using his forearm to wipe sweat and dust from his brow. The motion also blocked his eyes from Mike's stare. "Besides, nothing's set in stone yet. We're still thinking about what the next move should be. Maybe going out there for the summer if Morgan can get coverage for the bakery."

"That's fine. But you owe it to the guys and Devon to give them a heads-up. Even if it's only a maybe. Because I think it's actually more than that." Mike snapped the tile along his score mark. He chucked the cut-off section into the pile of debris in the corner hard enough that it shattered into a million pieces.

As the Powertools foreman in every sense, Mike was too wise for games.

"Okay, I'll tell them by the end of the week."

"Do better than that." Mike turned and glared. Could it be that carrying the weight of Joe's secret was crushing him too?

"Fine. Next time we take a break or something." Joe scrunched his eyes closed.

This was going to suck.

"Team meeting!" Mike bellowed, then grabbed Joe by the scruff of his T-shirt and dragged him into the stripped-down kitchen. Their current build was an old Victorian. It reminded him of the summer they'd spent renovating the house next to the one Kate had inherited from her grandfather. They'd gotten so lucky, meeting her then and seeing what the future could hold for them all. And had for many peaceful years.

Would his desire to evolve wreck all of that as sure as demolition day on a site like this?

Joe struggled to breathe, and not because of the manual labor he'd been doing that morning, tearing down the walls of this old house so they could rebuild them better. Stronger. Maybe that's what he needed to do for himself, and the crew.

As he stood there trying to get his shit together, Dave, Neil, James, and Devon joined them.

"What's this about?" Neil asked. "There's at least an hour and a half until lunchtime. Not that I'm complaining. It's getting hot out. We're going to need some fans in here soon."

Devon handed him a thermos, and for a minute they stood there breathing hard and chugging ice-cold water. It did nothing to cool Joe off. Not knowing what was coming.

"Joe has something he wants to share." Mike elbowed him in the ribs.

"Looks more like there's something you want him to say." Dave arched a brow at Joe, his gray eyes turning stormy as the gravity of the situation sank in, smothering the satisfaction they got from making progress on a job like their current one.

Joe drew a deep, if shaky breath, then said, "I'm thinking about going to Middletown."

"So?" Neil asked, lifting his hands and letting them slap his jeans below his tool belt. "It's kind of a regular thing these days. Have fun—"

"For a month. At least." Joe sighed, just saying it out loud easing some of the weight that had been compressing his chest for too long now. "Probably the whole summer, if we can swing it."

"This is going to be a hell of a lot of work." James looked around at the mountain of shit they had left to do. "But we can manage without you if you want a break. No problem."

"Why does this sound like more than a visit?" Devon wasn't accusatory, just curious. Figured that she would see right through him.

"It might be." Joe shrugged. Honestly, the only thing holding him back from committing was the group of people standing in an arc around him right then. If it weren't for the crew, he'd have already pulled the trigger on the house rental agreement he had completed and saved on his laptop. "Truth is, uh, Eli offered me a job. A good one."

"What?" Dave looked like someone had kicked him in the nuts.

"Yeah. Turns out Sally is pregnant." Joe wished the Hot Rods had told the crew themselves, but Eli had insisted the news should come from Joe directly along with the rest of the implications the situation had. Hell, he'd probably been talking to Mike since they'd both been pestering him to do this. But standing there, saying these things to the crew, and watching the mixture of disbelief, betrayal, and anger that flickered over their faces along with their other emotions...

It gutted him.

Devon softened a bit at that. "A baby? Oh, Joe. Of course you want to be there for that. I don't blame you. That's such great news."

"So you're, what? Going to be the kid's nanny?" Dave crossed his arms. They had always been best friends. "And why the fuck didn't you say so before?"

"I should have, sorry." Joe winced. "I wasn't trying to hide anything from you guys, it's just that this is...hard. I can't figure out the right thing to do."

James stepped up, put his hand on Joe's elbow and shot Dave a ferocious glare as he stood shoulder to shoulder with Joe. "You're really struggling being apart from Eli and Tom. I've seen it. We all have. It's a rough place to be in, living in two worlds."

"There's more," Mike prodded.

"So, yeah, Eli decided that Hot Rods isn't big enough for all of them anymore. Not with their family growing again. He wants me to design a new place for them and oversee the construction. Kyra, Ollie, and Van want a house at Hot Rides, too. They're both major projects."

"Hang on." Dave swiped at his mouth with the back of his hand. "You're saying you'd be the foreman. With what crew?"

"I guess one I'd have to hire out there?" Joe swallowed hard. It felt wrong, even to him, even for the good of his family, to think about working with anyone but the Powertools he'd built this business with for the past two decades.

"I get it now. You have a big fucking head." Dave flung out his arms, his mammoth fist nearly catching Joe's jaw in the process. "You're too good to be one of us and need to be the boss instead? Is this some kind of shitty midlife crisis or what?"

He winced, especially considering he'd had the same doubts initially. Only now, it seemed like so much more to him than that. Especially since Morgan agreed and encouraged his aspirations. "That's not it at all."

"Of course it isn't," Dave huffed.

Joe tried not to lose his cool, but a man could only take so much shit. Especially when making this decision was killing him. He didn't take it lightly. "Did it fucking look like that the other night when I practically begged Mike to fuck me?"

Joe strode to Dave and put his hands on the other guy's shoulders. "I want to do this for my family. And is it a challenge? Yeah, that too. Plus, we've outgrown our apartment, and Nathan wants a dog that we don't even have a yard for. He and Klea deserve to know their cousin, too. There are lots of reasons this makes sense. Not one of them is because I feel like I've outgrown anything here or that I'm better than you guys. Come on. You know that's not true, don't you?"

Mike stepped between them, deescalating the situation before someone got knocked flat on their ass. "I know one way to prove it. If you're still up for it."

Joe blinked, and suddenly he was. His body raged against the implication that he didn't give a shit about the crew when loving these people had damn near shredded his guts for the past year and might still in the year to come. He reached around Mike to grab Dave's hand and brought it to his crotch.

There was no way his friend could miss the raging erection he had from just thinking about where this was headed. Because all of them could agree on that. It was better to fuck it out than fight it out.

11

It shocked Joe when Dave wrenched his hand from Joe's dick as if scorched. Was he really that pissed that he would turn away in the face of Joe's obvious arousal? He spun on his heel and lumbered from the room, too fast for his gait to be completely smooth given his old injury.

"Where the hell do you think you're going?" Mike shouted after him.

But they didn't have to wait long to find out. He was only out of the room for a few seconds before they heard him grunt and trundle back in their direction after raiding the first-floor master, which they hadn't yet demoed.

Dave charged into the newly opened-up kitchen and living room area carrying a mattress on one shoulder like it was nothing. He dumped it on the floor where it bounced with a curious wobble. Neil grabbed a drop cloth from their pile of supplies in the corner and tossed it over the mattress.

"So romantic," Devon teased as she unhooked her tool belt before setting it carefully aside.

But Joe was under no misconceptions. This wasn't about romance. It was about something more primal than that—reaffirming the connection he shared with the crew and reassuring them that it was as important to him now as ever—even if he had to take a different path from them for a while.

He still didn't fully understand how things would work out, but there was the chance that life could be different after this experiment.

And if it was, he wanted to show them, one more time, how much they meant to him.

Morgan would approve. Hell, she'd been telling him to do this for days. She knew his heart and his fears and what would alleviate them. Besides, their long-standing agreement was that if he played with the crew, the next time they were all together he'd make it up by letting her be the center of their attention—something he enjoyed just as much as what was about to go down.

"What are you waiting for?" Mike asked, as if there was even a sliver of a chance Joe was going to bail on them right then and there. Not happening.

"Savoring the anticipation." He grinned and shucked his jeans as his friends did the same, though it was with a mix of regret, longing, and a nearly painful level of excitement that never dulled.

In that moment, the only thing Joe wanted was to show the crew what he'd never be able to say adequately. He was one of them, no matter where he went. What if they replaced him? Gave away both his work and his spot in their group to someone else? Maybe they would forget him and their friendship would fade away into nothing.

Now was his chance to show them that he didn't intend for that to happen.

Neil was naked first and practically dove onto the mattress on his back. He planted his feet on the bed and beckoned to James, his fingers curling toward his palm. James took a packet of lube from the pocket of his jeans, having learned a long time ago to be prepared for exactly this sort of spontaneous break-time loving.

While Devon undressed more slowly, studying her husbands as they teased each other, James got to work. He dove between Neil's legs and swallowed his partner's half-hard cock in a single gulp. Neil's hand speared into James's hair and held him close as he did his best to get Neil ready in record time. His gaze flicked upward at Joe, as if to ask what he was waiting for.

So he stripped off his shirt and edged closer to the mattress, a little unsure of how best to show his crewmates everything that was in his heart. Mike approached, humming in appreciation at the show James and Neil were putting on for their benefit. His fist stroked his cock even as Dave edged nearer also. Dave reached out, replacing Mike's fingers.

So Mike returned the favor, reaching over to Joe to do the same.

Joe raised his gaze, up, up, to meet Dave's, and when they collided, he extended his hand and wrapped it around Dave's cock as best he could. Damn, the guy was hung. It never ceased to amaze him, especially not now as he rubbed and worked Dave's shaft until it firmed in his grip. Dave sighed, and some of the tension in his frame eased as he settled into Joe's hold. The three of them—Mike, Joe, and Dave—jerked each other off as James finished getting Neil ready.

When Neil tugged James's hair, his cock left his husband's mouth with a wet noise that was unmistakably drenched in sex. Devon purred and crawled closer until she sat, now nude, on her heels at their sides. She claimed the lube from James and ripped it open with her teeth before drizzling it onto Neil's cock and massaging it in.

Then Neil nudged James's side until he turned. He grabbed James's hips, which were nearly as narrow as Devon's, and guided him down so that he practically sat on Neil. Before he got quite that far, Devon took Neil in her fist and raised his cock so it was standing straight up. Without so much as a word, James fit himself to Neil and sank down onto his dick, gasping at the familiar intrusion. His own cock was hard, waving between his legs as he began to grind on Neil.

Dave shuddered, his erection growing in Joe's hold.

Devon straddled both of her husbands then, aligning her pussy with James's dick and mounting him. James let them work him over, Neil fucking up into him from below as Devon rode him from above. In his happy place, James looked up at the three men stroking each other as they towered over him and licked his lips.

"Damn, you're hot," he told them even as he allowed himself to be the conduit for his partners' burgeoning pleasure.

"So are you." Mike's voice grew husky and his dick leaked into Dave's hand, which spread the glistening precome across his flesh.

Before Joe realized what was happening, Dave's cock fell from his grasp as the other guy knelt beside Neil, James, and Devon, leaning over them to make a bridge back to Mike and Joe. He opened his mouth and took Mike inside, as if touching him with his hands wasn't enough anymore.

Joe stood and stared. But when he strangled his own

cock and stroked it in time to Dave's movements, the other guy growled around Mike's shaft and swatted Joe's hand away.

"Hey, watch what you're smacking," Joe grumbled. Was Dave still pissed?

Dave only rolled his eyes, then abandoned Mike, who groaned, in order to engulf Joe's cock in his hot, wet mouth instead.

"Ah, fuck." Mike put one hand on Dave's shoulder, while Neil, James, and Devon began to rock below them. "Yeah. Show him how much you're going to miss him. Make sure he can't forget us."

Dave sucked the hell out of Joe's cock, doing things with his mouth that had Joe squirming. His tongue and lip piercings added an edge that did nothing to strengthen what little self-control Joe had around the crew. When it got too dangerous, too good, Dave swapped, alternating sucking on Mike and Joe while Neil, Devon, and James put on one hell of a show for them.

Joe extended his hand toward Dave, but with the trio at their feet, he couldn't reach the other man's dick anymore.

"James, you know you're jealous as fuck that Dave's got Joe's cock halfway down his throat." Mike fixed the problem, as he usually did. "Why don't you take care of him? If you can still think while Neil and Devon are blowing your mind."

James blinked up at them then. When he turned his head toward Dave, he smiled, but only for a moment, because then he filled his mouth with one of his favorite things, a nice hard cock.

Of all of them, only James was pro enough to handle Dave when he was fully erect, and he did his damnedest to engulf the man even if he sometimes lost control while being bounced around between his two lovers.

Dave's cock never left James's mouth for long, though. Maybe one or two glides across his lips or nose before James reclaimed him, sucking twice as hard to keep his prize the next time.

Joe let the energy they generated seep into his muscles and deeper to his soul. He seared the feeling into his memory, vowing to take it with him no matter where he went. He stroked Dave's shoulder and leaned into Mike's side when the foreman put his arm around Joe's waist to steady him upright.

Dave made a strangled sound as James devoured him and he did the same to them. He was obviously going through something because eventually he let go of Mike's cock long enough to say, "Joe, why don't you put your cock to better use?"

"Are you sure?" Joe didn't want there to be any confusion. This wasn't about him having to be in control, and Dave giving it up to him wasn't going to fix whatever was driving him to be closer to the Hot Rods branch of his family tree. "I swear that's not what this is."

"Shut up and fuck me already." Dave groaned. "If you're going to leave, you can at least be close to me like that one more time."

Shit! Joe's heart twisted. "I'm only going two states away, not to the moon. You guys can come visit as much as you want and we'll do our best to get back here too, although it's going to be tough if I'm managing the builds."

Everyone slowed and their cries quieted a bit at that.

"Enough talking." Mike put his hand over Joe's mouth, cutting off his air supply, keeping him from increasing the agony on Dave's face by pointing out how strained things could get. "Give him what he asked for."

Joe nodded and wrenched free of Mike's hold. He sank down beside Dave, then took the lube James pressed into his hand and slathered his cock with it. Dave was a gentle giant. Joe would never risk hurting the other man. Not like this, and not like he obviously already had, even if unintentionally. "I'm going to make you feel so good, Dave. I swear. I'll do the best I can for you."

Dave nodded, then returned to Mike's cock to distract himself. Mike fisted his hand in Dave's hair and used the grip to slowly and steadily fuck Dave's mouth. James reached up and played with Mike's balls, making the foreman grunt and force himself deeper between Dave's lips.

Joe couldn't resist the sight and sounds of his best friends enjoying each other so thoroughly. He put pressure on Dave's body until it began to open for him, taking him inside inch by inch. His ass was hot and tight around Joe's cock, gripping him as if he didn't plan to let him go, not then or ever.

"Shit, yes." Joe banded his arms around Dave, crushing the man to his chest as he embedded himself fully, then gave him some time to adjust to being filled.

Dave took a break from sucking and panted as Mike tapped the wet head of his cock against Dave's parted lips.

"Incredible, isn't it?" James asked in short pants between long pulls on Dave's dick. When Dave made a sound between a whimper and a strangled groan, James suckled him, swirling his tongue around the most sensitive parts of Dave's shaft until he seemed to regroup.

Dave pressed his ass back against Joe's abdomen so Joe began to fuck with slow, shallow movements that warmed them both up. Maybe a little too much, too fast. Because Joe was suddenly afraid he wasn't going to last long. Not with Dave's body welcoming him despite his desire to leave, and not with the sights and sounds of Neil, James, and Devon obviously getting off on watching them together, for what might be their final performance.

Fuck! He looked up at Mike, practically begging for help.

Mike growled and slid his dick from Dave's mouth. He brushed moisture from the edge of the other man's lips with his thumb and said, "I think Joe needs this more right now, if you want him to really fuck you well."

"Yeah. Let him have it then." Dave grunted when Joe jerked, slamming his hips into the guy's ass, unable to stop himself from giving Dave everything he had.

Mike settled behind Joe, putting his hands on Joe's waist to slow him down, keep his strokes into Dave's ass measured and smooth. Joe backed away from the precipice he'd been racing headlong toward, unable to brake on his own. And when Mike's cock nudged his ass, his hands clamped on Dave's shoulders, curling around them to anchor himself between the two men who'd been such huge parts of his life, and always would be.

In that moment, as Mike fused himself to Joe and sandwiched him between hot, hard walls of muscle, Joe realized the truth. This bond was unbreakable. Distance and time meant nothing compared to this. Whenever they came together, it would be just as powerful as if he'd spent every minute slaving over a job with them that week or not.

They would make this work. Even if it wasn't as often as they'd like.

"Remember when you thought this wasn't your

thing?" Mike rasped in Joe's ear as he penetrated with a single stroke, bottoming out in Joe's ass. His hand snaked around to plant itself on Joe's chest, his thumb flicking over the hard nipple there, making Joe's dick twitch in Dave's ass. "Tell us that it is. That it always will be."

"The crew is my thing!" Joe shouted. "I need you. All of you."

"Good." Mike tightened his arm around Joe's chest, making him feel surrounded by strength that he desperately needed lately and would in the weeks to come. "Don't forget it when you're far away. Remember this."

Joe grunted as Mike fucked into him a little harder and with less finesse than usual. "Don't let me go. Please."

"I won't. Ever," Mike promised.

For a while, Joe lost himself to the sensation of being pinned between two of the people he loved most in the world, letting Mike screw him tight to Dave, his body being used by them both to find indescribable pleasure.

And as Dave began to moan louder and louder, James shifted so that while he was pinned between Devon and Neil, much like Joe was between Dave and Mike, he could crane his neck to take more of Dave's fat cock. His talented fingers hovered near Dave's balls.

Dave groaned. "If you do that..."

"Yeah, do that," Mike ordered. "And when Dave falls, he's going to take us all with him. Ready?"

James opened his mouth wider and Dave fed him his cock. The clear expert on blowjobs, James treated Dave to his best, sucking, licking, deep throating, and bobbing even while Neil thrust into him hard enough to mash his face to Dave's abs. Devon held them both down, grinding on them to satisfy her own cravings.

Joe hugged Dave tight, his cock steely hard where it was buried in his friend's body. And when Dave jerked in his hold, he figured he'd tapped the other guy's prostate. So he aimed for it again and again. Mike bit Joe's shoulder and did the same, hammering into Joe with relentless accuracy.

Joe's cock flared, and Dave lost it.

He pumped his come down James's throat, shouting and cursing as he did. James swallowed furiously but still couldn't manage to drink it all, a tiny bead escaping to roll down his chin. Which obviously set the smaller guy off too. He stiffened between Devon and Neil, who both arched and spasmed, coming hard and long.

"Now," Mike insisted in Joe's ear as he ramped his fucking to a furious pace. "Join them. Show them what they do to you and how much you're going to miss this. Come, Joe. Now."

Joe did. He surrendered to the moment and the energy flowing through each of them, a connection that could never be severed. He pumped his seed deep into Dave's still-clenching ass and shot twice as hard when he felt Mike start to flood him as well.

Joe shook and rode the swell of rapture for so long he damn near blacked out. After he crested and began to float down the other side of his orgasm, he could only think about how hard he was going to come again when he recounted their session to Morgan later. She got off on hearing about their guy-time just as much as he did experiencing it for himself. Maybe more.

She was going to be ravenous, and he would take care of her precisely like he had Dave and the crew had done for each other. It was a beautiful symbiotic relationship that he was terrified he'd just ended.

When Mike slipped from Joe's body, Joe did the same from Dave's with one last bear hug to make letting go less difficult. Neil, James, and Devon made room for them on the mattress so they could collapse in a heap of bodies and limbs that should have been uncomfortable but definitely was not.

Dave clapped Joe on the shoulder. "I'm sorry for what I said when I was horny."

Joe burst out laughing despite the grief seeping in to undermine his relaxation.

"Dude, that was one hell of a terror boner." Devon sank deeper into Neil's and James's embraces. "It's going to be weird as fuck without Joe around, and we all know it. It's okay to admit it as long as you're still happy for him too."

"I'm sorry, guys. I swear this hurts me most. But I can't see any other way to make things work for now."

"Family is important. I get that." Dave shook Joe a bit then. "Just don't forget the rest of yours. We might not be blood, but we've been through some shit together, and that counts for something."

"A hell of a lot." Joe nodded. "I wish there was some way I could have both."

"Life is made up of hard choices," James leaned the side of his face on top of Devon's head. "No one is going to blame you for doing what you think is right."

"I'm still kind of pissed about it." Dave faux-glared. "But I'll probably get over it by the time you come visit next. And if not, I'm sure you'll figure out some way to make it up to me."

Joe shook his head, smiling. "I'll do my best."

12

"So the lease is signed then?" Mike asked as he sat with his elbows planted on his dining room table. His chin rested on his fists. It was hard to see his expression clearly with the late-day sun blasting through the window behind him, but Joe figured it wasn't all smiles. From her place beside him, opposite Joe, Kate put her hand on Mike's biceps.

"Yep, the official, finalized paperwork came through last night. Morgan is so excited. The kitchen in the place is massive and so is the yard. You'll have to come see it for yourself, but I have some pictures. Check it out. There's a guest room plus a sleeper sofa and another bathroom in the finished basement, which is going to make a great play area for the kids."

"Sounds like you'll have everything you need."

"Most things, but not all." Joe set his phone aside since Mike clearly wasn't interested in show-and-tell.

"Cut the shit." Mike let his hands fall forward, his palms smacking on the table. "This isn't a trip. It's a trial run."

"I guess it is. But I don't know if I can really go through with moving permanently. We'll have to see what it's like. This is a huge sacrifice for Morgan and me, and the kids."

"And the crew. We're going to miss you like hell. *I'm* gonna miss you." Mike sighed. "So know this... Whether you stay in Middletown three months or thirty years, we'll be here waiting for you if you ever decide to come back."

Joe spotted a familiar mop of curly brown hair bobbing as Abby peeked around the corner just then. *Oh shit.*

"What are you guys talking about?" Mike and Kate's daughter stared at them with big doe eyes that were equal parts horrified and disbelieving. It was just like the time she'd busted Joe playing Santa for the Powertools kids and figured out he wasn't real.

"Nothing meant for your ears," Mike advised her with the stern dad-tone he rarely broke out. "This is an adult conversation."

"Whatever, Dad. You tell me all the time that being a kid is no excuse. So tell me, Uncle Joe. Is it true? You're going away for the whole summer? Taking Nathan and Klea with you? And maybe never coming back? You're thinking of moving? Like for good?"

Joe felt the accusation in her stare stab him straight in the heart. He loved Abby and Landry as if they were his own kids. Hell, with as much time as she and Nathan spent together, she practically lived at his house as much as Kate and Mike's. "It's a possibility. Nothing is for sure yet. Well, except the summer part. That *is* happening."

"You wouldn't be taking Nathan and Klea with you if you didn't hope it sticks. I might be a kid, but I'm not stupid." She crossed her arms, her lower lip wobbling a bit despite the flush reddening her entire face. "Does Nathan know? Was he keeping this a secret from me too?"

Abby sent her parents a pitiful look that made Joe feel sorry for them. Damn it.

"Ah, no. Not yet. We didn't want the kids to get their hopes up until it was a done deal." Joe swallowed, wishing he could hug Abby or that someone would do the same for him so these agonizing moments hurt less. His doubts crashed over him as he swore he saw Abby lose faith in another cornerstone of her childhood. First Santa, now this.

Abby snorted, too wise for her age. "Yeah, right. He's going to freak out. How could you do this to us? Nathan is my best friend. I hate you, Uncle Joe. And so will Nathan when he figures out why you're bribing him. You can't buy his love with a dumb puppy."

She spun on the heel of her rainbow-striped socks and took off as Kate gasped.

In her wake, Mike growled a warning, "Abby!"

It didn't do any good. She raced down the hall, then slammed the door to her room.

The muffled sobs that filtered through the walls crushed a part of Joe's soul. He'd sworn to protect their kids, and here he was, breaking their little hearts.

"I'm so sorry, Joe." Kate rushed over to him and smothered him in a tight embrace. "Abby was out of line. I swear she's getting a head start on this teenager thing. She doesn't understand how complicated and difficult these kinds of decisions are despite the fact that she acts like she's twelve going on twenty-seven. I'll go talk to her. She *will* apologize to you. And someday, she and the rest of our kids will understand you're trying to do what's best for them."

Kate put her hands on her cheeks as she backed away, clearly mortified. While she slipped into Abby's room, Mike muttered a curse beneath his breath. "Sorry, man. I'm pretty sure she gets that temper from her mom. God help me if this isn't even peak-teenager drama yet."

Joe chuckled, but it stuck in his dry throat. "It's fine. Don't go too hard on her. I half expect Nathan is going to refuse to go with us, or maybe run away so he can come back here."

"If he does, you know I'll be waiting to let him in before I read him the riot act. He's welcome here any time. You're family. All of you." Mike rubbed his temple. "I'd offer to let him stay while you're working on this project, but we both know that isn't the point. You need to see if he can adapt. If any of us can."

Joe didn't bother to deny it. And if Mike had officially extended the invitation, it would have been too easy to take him up on it. Nathan and Abby were best friends, even now that they weren't so young anymore. Ripping them apart was going to wound more than just them. His own heart might never recover. But like Morgan had said, if that was the case, they could always come back. Just to somewhere other than their too-small apartment.

He drew a deep, if shaky, breath. "Thanks. Mike..."

"Yeah?"

"Am I being the most selfish motherfucker in the world?" Joe scrunched his eyes closed. Even now he still couldn't be sure he was doing the right thing.

"Nah, I don't think so." Mike reached out and put his hand on Joe's knee. "There's nothing wrong with wanting to be closer to Tom and Eli. They're your family too. So are the Hot Rods and Hot Rides gangs. We've known them damn near forever. And they need you now. Plus, you obviously need them."

"I can't really explain why. But...yeah, I do."

"You're likely to be in the running for godfather and not only uncle. Which is a great thing. So go, Joe." Mike stood then and walked to the window. He spread his legs and clasped his hands behind his back as he looked out onto the lawn outside, and the pool in the neighboring yard. The place where so many things had begun for them. And maybe where a few ended after today. "You know where to find us. We'll always be here for you."

"But what if you're not? Not here, I mean." A tiny wisp of hope rose in Joe like the smoke from Dave and Kayla's chimney had that night they welcomed him home. What if the rest of the Powertools could make a new place too...

"Of course we will be." Mike turned, his head cocked as if anything else was inconceivable.

Joe knew then that the crew wasn't yet ready to hear his greatest desire. And likely never would be.

If he and Morgan did this, they were doing it on their own. And that scared the shit out of him. But he'd never know how it would work out unless he tried it. Thinking about the other things in his life—like sharing with the crew—he would have missed out on if he hadn't been bold enough to attempt something new was the motivation he needed to take this first step.

"I guess I better go and tell the kids before Abby does it for me." Joe stood but couldn't quite force his boots to head for the door.

"Yeah, probably too late for that. Abby texts like her fingers are on fire. But at least you can do some damage control." Mike crossed the gap between them and slapped Joe on the back in a one-armed hug. "We've only ever wanted what's best for each other, so believe me when I say that right now, this is a good move for you. I've felt it coming for a while. It's okay, Joe. We won't love you any less if you live a few states over. Even if you root for their piece-of-shit football team instead of ours."

Joe laughed at that, but said seriously, "Don't worry. I'm never changing teams. I'm a Powertools guy for life."

"Good." Mike nodded, then lifted his chin toward the door. "Get out of here and take care of your family. I'm going to do the same."

Mike sighed and ambled toward Abby's room, where her crying had thankfully stopped as Joe saw himself out.

13

Morgan clasped Joe's hand as they made the familiar climb up the wooden stairs to Kayla and Dave's cabin. She let her fingers trail along the railing, soaking in the smoothness of the freshly applied stain as well as the smell of the springtime bringing the earth to life around them. She wanted to remember everything about this place and this night for the times ahead.

Joe must have felt the weight of the evening too. He paused before opening the door to turn toward her and kiss her gently. "You ready?"

"Yeah." Morgan smiled. "It feels almost like the first time again. I'm kind of nervous."

"Because you know what's coming now." Joe tucked her hair behind her ear. "I promised, cupcake. Tonight is going to be all about you."

"No, it's more than that." Morgan hugged Joe tight. "Knowing this might be our final shot—it's a lot of pressure. I want to show them, and you, how much I love

117

them. And how ready I am for this new adventure, even if I'm also sad and scared and..."

"God, I love you." This time Joe's kiss was more urgent.

And suddenly, they were both ready to charge through the door.

Except they didn't have to. Mike yanked it open and ushered them inside. "What the hell are you doing making out on the porch? Have you already forgotten how this works?"

Dave grumbled too. "Get in here and shut the door or I'm not going to be able to send you off in style, if you know what I mean."

"You could stand to shrink a few inches. You've got plenty to spare." James shook his head at Dave.

Joe and Morgan practically ran inside, and they didn't even bother with pleasantries before they looked at each other, grinned, and stripped.

"Well, hello to you too," Kayla joked, already nude where she was perched beside Dave.

What little anyone else was wearing vanished by the time Morgan turned around and faced the crew. She should probably be ashamed of how brazen she was, or how greedy, but they'd long ago erased any of those bullshit feelings she'd lived with before Joe...and the crew.

"You know, I can't say I mind all this—going away, welcome back, going away again." Neil shrugged. "The more you flit around, the more excuses we have to party. I'm not complaining about that."

"Unfortunately, there might not be another chance. At least not here, not with us all. Definitely not for a while." Joe swallowed hard. "So you better get it out of your system tonight."

"Then I guess you get to be the guest of honor since

you're getting promoted and all." Kate smiled at him. In crew-talk, that was code for being the person who got spoiled by everyone else, usually an honor and pleasure reserved for birthdays or special occasions or healing, when someone needed special attention.

Joe seemed to recognize that right then Morgan did. He always took care of her, and tonight was not going to be the exception to that rule.

"Actually, if you all don't mind..." Joe looked at Morgan and smiled sadly. "I want Morgan to have that experience since I feel shitty that she won't have the opportunity on her birthday or the rest of the summer at least."

"Are you sure?" Devon asked. "I'm pretty sure there's enough of us to do two things...or people...at once."

"Yeah." Joe turned to face Morgan fully then. "Years ago, this is what you told me you desired most, and I'm taking it away from you. You haven't complained once although I know it's a huge sacrifice. I'm not sure how I'm going to fix that yet, but...tonight..."

"Joe, you've given me everything I dreamed of so many times over." Morgan went onto her tiptoes and kissed him sweetly. Still, there was an edge to the exchange that guaranteed the night would be memorable. "There's no need to feel guilty about that."

"Even so..." Joe looked to the crew. "Will you do this, for me? Spoil my wife tonight, please."

Dave kissed Kayla, who nodded and shoved him toward Morgan and Joe. He smiled wolfishly as he stalked closer. Mike, James, and Neil weren't far behind.

"Hell yes, we will," Neil confirmed.

"And I'll help you do the same after," Joe promised.

"Don't worry, each of us will get ours later. At home."

Kate clinked her wine glass with Devon's and Kayla's. The three of them were grinning as they watched the crew circling Morgan. "You know sharing only turns them on more."

Besides, it wouldn't surprise her in the least if Kayla and Devon held each other over from the way they were cuddling, practically purring. Morgan grinned. Joe and the rest of the guys loved watching them together too. Win-win.

"Damn straight." Mike shot a grin in his wife's direction. If she'd been within arm's reach, he would certainly have smacked her ass. Instead, Morgan did it to Mike.

Normally, she was less bold than that, Kayla and Devon having a corner on the sassy of the group. But tonight she felt powerful, focusing the attention of the five men circling her.

Morgan looked up at Mike and asked, "Where do you want me, foreman?"

He smiled at her and dove in for a kiss. When his scruff rasped against her skin, harsher than Joe's touch, her eyes closed and she let him drink from her lips. Joe groaned and stroked his cock, which must have ached from getting so hard, so fast.

"Dave, get on the floor." Mike held out a hand and helped lever the big man down to the thick carpet in front of the fire. It was for the best with his leg, and he loved letting the women boss him around. Being the biggest of them, people often made assumptions. Maybe during the day and regular life, he was fine with living up to them. But here, with the crew, he relaxed and let them have their way with him for the most part.

Morgan planned to do just that. The instant he was

splayed out before her, she pounced on him, her palms landing on the muscles of his broad chest and kneading them.

Kayla hummed in the background, fully approving of Dave's shudder beneath Morgan. She cheered, "Get it, girl."

Morgan smiled as she mitigated the aggression of her approach with a long, deep kiss. Dave tasted different than Mike, but every bit as enticing. She bit his lower lip, then rocked over him, already impressed by the ridge of his cock. It had been a while since she'd had him inside her.

In that instant, she flashed back to one special time, nearly thirteen years before, when he'd given her a gift more precious than she could ever have dared ask for. And suddenly she couldn't wait to hold him within her again.

Morgan reached behind her to grab his cock and angle it enough that she could start fitting him into her body.

"Hey, wait." Dave grabbed her hips, holding her in place. "Are you sure you're ready for that so soon? I don't want to hurt you."

"She knows what she can handle." Joe stared down at her with pride in his gaze. "Let her have your dick if that's what she needs."

"Yeah, okay. Go for it." Dave's head dropped back on the carpet and his hands shifted to stroking her thighs instead of restraining her. While he did, Neil and James knelt on one side of her while Mike and Joe took up spots opposite from them.

They caressed her all over, her hair, her back, her ass, her arms, her breasts...everywhere. Ensuring that even if she hadn't already been soaked, she would have gotten there by the time Dave's dick began to stretch her open.

She only had half of him when she had to stop for a second, letting her body adjust to his intrusion. Beneath her, he was breathing hard, muttering about how damn good she felt hugging him.

"Ease up and then try again," James suggested, no stranger to taking the guys himself.

"No." Morgan shook her head. "Just needed a second."

She sank lower, gasping as Dave spread her impossibly wide.

"Don't act like you don't love it." Joe had turned into an entirely different man, someone even sexier and bolder and slightly less polite than usual when they played like this. And she couldn't say she minded. "Take his huge cock all the way inside you. I love watching your pussy stretch for him."

Morgan whimpered and did as her husband commanded. Because she enjoyed the hell out of it too, almost as much as she got off on watching his cock leak as he saw how damn much she enjoyed the attention of him and his four friends.

Any time they did this, it reminded Morgan of when the crew had fucked her and filled her with their seed in order to help them start a family. There were so many memories, all of them amazing, that she started to lose herself to the overwhelming emotion of them.

"Stop thinking so much," Mike ordered.

"I can't," Morgan cried out. What they were about to do, leave the security of the crew, was terrifying even if she believed to her bones that they should.

"Let me help you then." Mike blanketed her back. He fit the blunt head of his very lubed cock to her ass and began to work his way inside, just like he'd done to Joe the last time they'd played together. Knowing that he rode her the same way he did his partner and someone he respected made her accept his authority. It wasn't that he saw her as less-than. No. He saw her as strong enough to take him.

Mike breached her ass and pushed inside bit by bit, making Dave's head rock on the carpet.

"Can you feel him too?" she asked the big man beneath her, who made it okay for her to express her own pleasure and admit that it was intense without feeling weak.

"Fuck yeah." Dave looked over to Kayla then, who, sure enough, had Devon on her lap. They were making out while they watched their men being used to bring Morgan as much pleasure as possible.

Mike grunted and thrust particularly deep, possessing her fully and thrilling Dave in the process.

Morgan whimpered. It wasn't often she did this. In fact, she had believed she didn't get off on anal until the crew had shown her otherwise. It was extreme and shocking, just like being the recipient of their collective devotion.

When Mike began to move within her, Morgan beckoned James forward. The only woman he ever fucked, in their group or not, was Devon. But he never passed up a blowjob, and suddenly she wanted to be entirely filled with the crew, unable to deny that she'd cherish them always. No matter where they lived or worked. She wanted nothing more than to give each of them what they wanted most. To be what they needed like they had always been for her.

When she opened her mouth, he guided his erection

to her lips and flirted with poking inside. She licked him lightly, teasing him like he enjoyed. Neil leaned over and kissed James as she treated him to some of his own medicine. Watching the two of them make out always did incredible things to her libido. They were so graceful and raw at the same time; she could stare at them all day.

Immersed in their exchange, Neil inched closer. His cock prodded the side of her breast, and they both froze. Her pussy clamped around Dave, who latched onto James's thigh and squeezed. James looked down to see what was happening. He grinned. "Move over here, Neil."

James nudged Neil around until he knelt over Dave's head, giving the man buried deep in her pussy a spectacular view of Neil's balls and ass. But when James took the bottle of lube Mike handed him and drizzled it down the center of her chest, she knew where they were headed.

Mike wrapped his hands around her shoulders and lifted her more upright. She settled more fully onto Dave, driving him inside her to the root. When she moaned, James got to his feet then slid deep into her mouth. She sucked on his cock, drawing hard to comfort herself as her senses became overwhelmed with input.

Bombarded by rapture.

Then Neil was there, fitting his hard-on in place between her breasts, which he formed into pillows around his shaft. If he had any complaints about her boobs, he sure didn't show it. Instead he began to thrust between them. "Morgan, you have incredible tits. I love fucking them."

James smiled. "Do it, Neil."

He'd often told them how much he enjoyed when the crew women gave Neil things that he couldn't. And Devon was a bit too petite, including in the bust, to really pull it off. So Morgan was more than happy to let him use her. It felt good to her too, another sensation to add to the growing list. When she hummed, Neil and James came together again, making out more intensely than before.

It drew Morgan out of the haze of bliss they were creating around her when Neil stiffened and barked out a curse at the ceiling. It wasn't until she looked down and realized that Dave had lunged upward in some kind of crunch, his arms around Neil's hips, and buried his face in the other man's ass, eating furiously, that she realized what had happened.

She then glanced over at Joe, who had a wicked smile plastered on his handsome face as he stroked himself and took in every detail of the elaborate fucking going on before him.

Morgan moaned when Neil's grip tightened, creating a soft, fuckable tunnel that he made good use of, his balls slapping against Dave's chin when he did.

She shuddered, her pussy hugging Dave tighter, rewarding him for his assistance.

The entire time his friends thrilled her, Joe stood right there, supervising. His callused hands stroked his cock, which looked harder than she remembered seeing it, maybe ever. He groaned each time she quivered, turned on even more by the sight of her husband than the impressive things his friends could do to her body.

She twisted until James's cock slid along her cheek instead of inside her mouth.

"Will someone give Joe a hand with that?" Morgan asked even though she had to clear her throat twice to get the request out.

Always willing to assist, Kate waltzed over with a

sensual smile. "Let's see how well Kayla has taught me massage skills, huh?"

Standing behind Joe so as not to block his view, Kate dusted Joe's hand from his hard-on and replaced it with her own. He groaned. "Fuck, Kate. Yeah. Not too fast or I'm going to lose it."

"I hope you do." Morgan smiled up at him, her own body illuminated at every nerve ending she possessed. "Just make sure you let James have a taste. You know he loves that."

James's cock twitched, slapping her cheek lightly, so she slowly took him back into her mouth until her lips rested at the base of his shaft. He was just the right size to ensure she could really thrill him when she went down on him without risk of choking.

In the background, Morgan saw the fluid motion of Kayla and Devon scissoring as they kissed, obviously moved by their husbands' roles in making Morgan lose her mind in the best possible way.

The guys got serious then, working together to overwhelm her with ecstasy. She lost the ability to think rationally or do anything other than react to their caresses and thrusts. Their moans the only encouragement she needed to do more of what they each liked.

They fucked her relentlessly, driving her to so many orgasms that she lost count and her body began to give out. But when Dave's groan rumbled through her where they were joined, she knew the crew were almost spent too. She was about to satisfy five of the most virile men she knew, which would never cease to amaze and inspire her.

Morgan opened her eyes. "Come on, guys. With me

this time. In me. On me. Show me how you really feel about fucking me."

She'd barely spoken the words when Joe roared. "Thank God. Can't wait another second."

Kate's fingers flew over his cock, milking him as he drenched Morgan's chest and Neil's dick with an epic release. James hunched over to lick every drop from her skin before he returned and unloaded in her mouth.

And as Morgan swallowed, drinking from him, Mike stiffened behind her. He clamped her to his torso and pumped into her quickly, though not recklessly. When he grasped her hips and locked tight to her ass, she knew he was about to fill her with exactly what she'd asked for. Emotion along with ecstasy.

The first splash of his hot release inside her triggered her orgasm, a climax to top all the others that evening. She smothered Dave's cock with her pussy, forcing him to erupt also. She ground on him, her body pulsing around him as she took what she needed and simultaneously gave him what he craved.

She rode him until his come overflowed her and drained the last of her energy with it.

Utterly spent, she sagged.

Ten hands were there to catch her and lower her gently to the floor beside Joe, who wrapped himself around her protectively. He whispered soothing, loving things to her as their friends took care of them, cleaned them and covered them with a soft blanket. Then each man took turns kissing her before finding their own partners to cuddle with.

Someone dimmed the room lights to almost nothing as hushed whispers and sighs surrounded them. In the romantic amber flicker of the fire, Joe cradled her against his chest. "You were incredible, Morgan. The sexiest thing I've ever seen, never mind had the pleasure to touch. I swear we'll find a way. I don't know how, but...this can't be it."

Morgan kissed his jaw, unwilling to let him slip out of the peaceful place they both floated through together in wake of their monumental release. She laid her head on his shoulder, utterly wrecked, then murmured, "It's probably for the best. We could never top tonight. Thank you for giving me this. I love you."

"I love you too, cupcake. And I always will." Joe squeezed her. "No surprise there."

14

J oe sat in the driver's side of their car, which was jam packed with the kids and suitcases. In addition, they towed a small trailer of stuff. Their apartment had made them damn near minimalists, but they still managed to have more than he'd expected when it came time to pack.

If things went like he thought they might, this could be a one-way journey.

The rest of the crew along with Mike and Kate's kids had come to send them off. He couldn't quite bring himself to shut the door on them yet.

After a million hugs and well wishes, they were finally loaded up and ready to start a new phase of their lives. Nathan, who was on the side of the car where the Powertools were huddled together, rolled down his window.

"Be good for your dad, you hear?" Dave told him in a gentle murmur that made Joe's heart cramp. He hadn't even considered how the other guy would feel about being separated from the boy he'd literally created. Like the rest of the crew, he'd been a part of Nathan's whole life.

Nathan nodded and held his fist out the window so Dave could bump it like they always did when they saw each other.

Someone sniffled, but Joe couldn't look to see who or he'd say fuck it and start taking shit out of the car. Morgan reached over and rubbed his thigh.

"It's just for a few months. Not so different from how things have been lately with you going back and forth, except maybe that we'll get to come hang out with you instead of you visiting them." Mike nodded once and clapped Joe on the shoulder next to his seatbelt.

"Yeah, we'll be out for Kyra, Ollie, and Van's engagement party at the end of the month." James smiled.

"Actually, it's twenty-seven days." Figured Abby knew the exact number. Joe wouldn't put it past her and Nathan to be keeping a countdown clock that tallied it to the second. Nathan hadn't exploded like Abby, but he'd sulked hard for days after learning they were going to be spending a season apart. Joe wasn't so sure the kids would tolerate it for longer than that. Or if he and Morgan could do it either.

One thing he did know: "I'll be glad to see you all again then. No matter how far apart we are, you'll always be with me."

"And you'll be one of the crew," Mike promised.

"Not as big a part of the crew as Dave, mind you..." Neil joked before Devon smacked him in the gut with the back of her knuckles. Everyone stared at him until he shrugged. "Sorry. I suck at feelings except when I'm kidding around. I'm gonna miss the fuck out of you. You know that, right?"

Landry's eyes got wide as he took in his honorary uncle dropping the mac-daddy curse.

Ordinarily Joe would laugh. Instead, he clenched his jaw to hold in a wail. He didn't bother trying to respond. Instead he slung his arm around Neil's shoulder as the guy leaned in and gave him a single squeeze before clapping his back. "I already miss you guys. I just..."

"This is what you need to do." Mike nodded. "That's fine. We understand. We're not going anywhere."

Joe winced, because he wished they were. Not that he would ask them to uproot their entire lives—their businesses, their kids, everything—just for his convenience, but if he could have anything he desired, it would be that. To keep his family, in the broadest sense of the word, whole.

Because forfeiting one giant part of himself to fill another void seemed like a brutal tradeoff.

Mike leaned on the frame of the car, peering in with a wince at the cramped space overflowing with their most important belongings. He scrubbed it away and replaced it with a terrible attempt at a reassuring smile for Morgan and the kids. "You know this ain't a one-way street. You get out there and change your minds, turn around. Come home."

But for the first time in a while, Joe didn't know where exactly that was. He was lost.

Totally screwed.

Yet heading off anyway to try to get his bearings and figure things out.

"Thanks, Mike. And...I'm sorry."

"No need for that shit."

"Uncle Mike said a bad word," Klea whisper-shouted to Morgan. "But not as bad as Uncle Neil."

Mike didn't stop to ask for forgiveness. He held his hand out, and waited for Joe to shake it before saying, "The crew is for life. We'll figure this out. Just take care of yourself and your family, until we're all together again to watch your back like you do ours."

"Will do." Joe turned the key in the ignition. If he didn't pull away soon, he wasn't going to be able to do it at all.

Mike nodded and stepped back, shutting the car door with a *thunk* that sounded too final.

Joe glanced up and saw the rest of the crew—Devon, Kayla, and Kate included—fanned out in a horseshoe behind Mike. Devon had her head on James's shoulder and Dave knuckled one eye before Kayla put a reassuring hand on his back. As much as teetering on the verge of making this leap was agonizing for Joe, it was equally so for his friends, and his family.

Nathan rolled up his window but Abby broke free of Kate to rush over and put her hand on the glass. Nathan matched it on the other side.

Joe's soul withered. He mashed the brake to the floor and reached for the keys to turn off the car, but Morgan encased his fingers with hers. For his ears only, she murmured, "We're with you. I know we're not the same as having the entire crew, but we support you because I really believe it's best for us. You deserve this opportunity. We all do. Let's go."

Then she raised her voice and tipped her head toward the backseat. "Hey, Nathan, Klea. Did you know that at our new place, there's a whole area just for you guys to play that's not in your rooms? Dad ordered a projector so we can show movies real big on the wall and have popcorn while we watch. And Uncle Quinn said he found a dirt bike just the right size to show you how to ride on your own in our big backyard. How cool is that?"

"Seriously?" Nathan whipped his gaze toward the front of the car, his hand slipping a bit off Abby's. Mike lifted his daughter into his arms and hugged her, tucking her face into the crook of his neck. She might have been getting a little too old for that, but she didn't fight him. Joe realized that whether or not they stayed, nothing remained the same forever. "That's so cool! Can I paint it green like the one in the racing show?"

"Absolutely." Morgan smiled at him. "I'm sure your uncle Eli will be so happy to have you nearby that he'll be glad to help you with it. Or sweet-talk Aunt Sally into doing it, I should say."

Joe snorted. And there it was. The future they were hoping for. He could never make it a reality if he didn't do this now. He put the car in gear, then sat up straighter.

He rolled down the window and said, "We'll see you soon. One way or another. I promise."

"Gonna hold you to that. Now get out of here." Mike lifted his hand in a wave that the rest of the crew mimicked, each of them calling goodbye or shouting their love.

Right before Joe pulled away, he heard Abby's quivering voice cry out, "Uncle Joe, I don't hate you. I'm sorry I said that."

He turned and blew her a kiss. "I love you too, Abby. So much. I promise we'll have you and Landry out to visit as soon as possible, okay?"

"Promise?" she blinked at him.

"Promise."

Abby settled with her head on Mike's shoulder and

waved. Unable to prolong their parting any longer, Joe did it. He left.

As they turned out onto their sleepy street, then along the country roads, and out across the state toward Middletown and their fate, Morgan never once let go of Joe's knee.

"Daddy?" Nathan asked a while later.

Joe cleared his throat and answered, "Yeah?"

"I'm sorry you're sad." He looked at his sister. "I promise we're going to be good. I'm just glad we're going to be together this time. I bet Uncle Eli and Great Uncle Tom will make you feel better when we get to Middletown."

"You know what, son? You're right." Joe blinked a few times to unblur his eyes, then focused on the road ahead instead of looking in the rearview mirror. There had to be a way to make this work for everyone—including the rest of the crew—and he was going to find it even if it took a while and a ton of work. "You know what else will help?"

"What?" Nathan asked.

"Your new puppy."

"You mean it?" Nathan perked up, and Klea set her tablet playing cartoons aside to stare at Joe with big gorgeous eyes that looked so much like Morgan's.

"Yeah, buddy. There was a litter born at the construction site. Uncle Bryce is looking after them and thinking about keeping one for himself. But he said you can have your pick first."

"Really?" Nathan's eyes grew wide and Klea high-fived him.

"Do you think I could name it?" she asked her brother, who was a perfect little man, always looking out for her even though she didn't really need him to. Joe knew that feeling well.

"Yeah, definitely." Nathan beamed. "And we can take him for walks and play fetch in the yard." Then he hesitated. "But what will happen at the end of the summer? What if there's no room for the puppy when we go home?"

Joe looked to Morgan then, and she fielded the question, delicately as ever. "No matter what happens over the next couple of months, things are going to be different afterward. Remember? We talked about it."

"Are we coming back at all?" Klea asked, making Joe aware just how damn intuitive she was.

"We don't know yet, pumpkin," he answered honestly. "We have to see how things go."

"But even if we do, it will be to a new, bigger house with plenty of space for your dog. I swear," Morgan told the kids. Then she reminded them, "None of those things are as important as knowing that wherever we end up, we'll have each other. Right?"

"Right." Klea nodded, then settled into her seat, picking up her tablet and clicking play on her video, apparently satisfied.

Nathan spent the next two hours straight talking about how much he loved the puppy he hadn't even met yet. Morgan flipped through her phone, saving ideas for merchandizing a bakeshop nook inside Devra's restaurant in addition to drafting recipes she thought would complement Devra's menu. And Joe felt lighter than he had in a while, reminding himself that the crew would be taking this same road out to see them in less than a month. A month that was going to be filled with interesting and intense new work that would make the time fly by.

With every mile they drove, he smiled a little more.

Maybe, just maybe, they weren't as screwed as he'd thought.

~

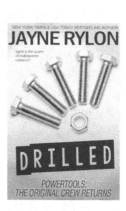

TO KEEP READING about the crew's adventures, check out the next book in the Powertools: The Original Crew Returns series, Drilled, by clicking HERE.

If you'd like to start at the very beginning with the Powertools Crew, you can download a discounted boxset of the first six books HERE.

Yes, I know it says complete series but I wrote a seventh book more recently and haven't gotten around to updating the boxset yet, sorry!

You can find the seventh Powertools book, More the Merrier, HERE.

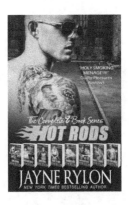

If you missed out on the Powertools: Hot Rods series, you can buy all eight books in a discounted single-volume boxset by clicking HERE.

To read more about the Hot Rides gang, starting with Quinn, Trevon, and Devra's story, Wild Ride, click HERE.

CLAIM A $5 GIFT CERTIFICATE

Jayne is so sure you will love her books, she'd like you to try any one of your choosing for free. Claim your $5 gift certificate by signing up for her newsletter. You'll also learn about freebies, new releases, extras, appearances, and more!

www.jaynerylon.com/newsletter

WHAT WAS YOUR FAVORITE PART?

Did you enjoy this book? If so, please leave a review and tell your friends about it. Word of mouth and online reviews are immensely helpful and greatly appreciated.

JAYNE'S SHOP

Check out Jayne's online shop for autographed print books, direct download ebooks, reading-themed apparel up to size 5XL, mugs, tote bags, notebooks, Mr. Rylon's wood (you'll have to see it for yourself!) and more.
www.jaynerylon.com/shop

LISTEN UP!

The majority of Jayne's books are also available in audio format on Audible, Amazon and iTunes.

ABOUT THE AUTHOR

 Jayne Rylon is a *New York Times* and *USA Today* bestselling author who has sold more than one million books. She has received numerous industry awards including the Romantic Times Reviewers' Choice Award for Best Indie Erotic Romance and the Swirl Award, which recognizes excellence in diverse romance. She is an Honor Roll member of the Romance Writers of America. Her stories used to begin as daydreams in seemingly endless business meetings, but now she is a full time author, who employs the skills she learned from her straight-laced corporate existence in the business of writing. She lives in Ohio with her husband, the infamous Mr. Rylon, and their cat, Frodo. When she can escape her purple office, she loves to travel the world, avoid speeding tickets in her beloved Sky, SCUBA dive, hunt Pokemon, and–of course–read.

Jayne Loves To Hear From Readers
www.jaynerylon.com
contact@jaynerylon.com
PO Box 10, Pickerington, OH 43147

facebook.com/jaynerylon

twitter.com/JayneRylon

instagram.com/jaynerylon

youtube.com/jaynerylonbooks

bookbub.com/profile/jayne-rylon

amazon.com/author/jaynerylon

ALSO BY JAYNE RYLON

More the Merrier *NEW*

POWERTOOLS: HOT RODS

Powertools Spin Off. Keep up with the Crew plus...

Seven Guys & One Girl. Enough Said?

King Cobra

Mustang Sally

Super Nova

Rebel on the Run

Swinger Style

Barracuda's Heart

Touch of Amber

Long Time Coming

POWERTOOLS: HOT RIDES

Powertools and Hot Rods Spin Off.

Menage and Motorcycles

Wild Ride

Slow Ride

Hard Ride

Joy Ride

Rough Ride

POWERTOOLS: RETURN OF THE CREW

The original crew is back with more steamy menage stories!

Screwed

Drilled

Grind

Pound

MEN IN BLUE

Hot Cops Save Women In Danger

Night is Darkest

Razor's Edge

Mistress's Master

Spread Your Wings

Wounded Hearts

Bound For You

DIVEMASTERS

Sexy SCUBA Instructors By Day, Doms On A Mega-Yacht By Night

Going Down

Going Deep

Going Hard

STANDALONE

Menage

Middleman

Nice & Naughty

Contemporary

Where There's Smoke

Report For Booty

COMPASS BROTHERS

Modern Western Family Drama Plus Lots Of Steamy Sex

Northern Exposure

Southern Comfort

Eastern Ambitions

Western Ties

COMPASS GIRLS

Daughters Of The Compass Brothers Drive Their Dads Crazy And Fall In Love

Winter's Thaw

Hope Springs

Summer Fling

Falling Softly

COMPASS BOYS

Sons Of The Compass Brothers Fall In Love

Heaven on Earth

Into the Fire

Still Waters

Light as Air

PLAY DOCTOR

Naughty Sexual Psychology Experiments Anyone?

Dream Machine

Healing Touch

RED LIGHT

A Hooker Who Loves Her Job

Complete Red Light Series Boxset

FREE - Through My Window - FREE

Star

Can't Buy Love

Free For All

PICK YOUR PLEASURES

Choose Your Own Adventure Romances!

Pick Your Pleasure

Pick Your Pleasure 2

RACING FOR LOVE

MMF Menages With Race-Car Driver Heroes

Complete Series Boxset

Driven

Shifting Gears

PARANORMALS

Vampires, Witches, And A Man Trapped In A Painting

Paranormal Double Pack Boxset

Picture Perfect

Reborn

PENTHOUSE PLEASURES

Naughty Manhattanite Neighbors Find Kinky Love

Taboo

Kinky

Sinner

Mentor

ROAMING WITH THE RYLONS

Non-fiction Travelogues about Jayne & Mr. Rylon's Adventures

Australia and New Zealand